CHASING DANGER

RUTHLESS EMPIRE

BOOK TWO

BY EVIE RILEY

Chasing Danger

An MM Mafia Romance

Ruthless Empire

Book Two

Copyright © 2024

Evie Riley

Second Edition

ISBN: 978-1-77357-679-4

Published by Naughty Nights Press LLC

Cover Art By CDG Cover Designs

CHASING DANGER

A surprising connection.
A risky lifestyle.
A true history revealed.

In a cozy coffee shop, flamboyant barista Oliver Grant uses his bubbly demeanor and flamboyant clothing to distract from the scars on his face and his belief that he is unlovable. What starts as casual conversations with a mysterious man over coffee becomes more as shared passions for classic cinema and art spark a deep connection.

Drawn by the perfect cup of coffee, D'Angelo Bianchi is unexpectedly captivated by a younger man's vibrant personality and exceptional latte art. When an attack linked to his mafia ties threatens Oliver's safety, the broody man's protective instincts kick in, revealing a hidden heart of gold. As their relationship deepens, their bond is tested by additional threats and escalating violence.

Can their desire survive the ruthless dangers of D'Angelo's world?

An intoxicating blend of passion, danger, and heartfelt romance, Chasing Danger is book two in a fierce world of gay male mafia romance. While interconnected, the books in this series can be enjoyed standalone.

CHAPTER ONE

D'Angelo

A DEAD BODY lay in my bed.

That fact wasn't particularly shocking, since I was the one who killed the man. Their identity, however, was a surprise.

I'd known Shane for only a few weeks after picking him up at one of my own clubs. He'd been a satisfactory lover, and most importantly, he'd been available whenever I wanted. My schedule kept me busy, so meeting up at odd hours for a quick fuck was commonplace.

After a long night dealing with a new drug shipment, I'd just wanted to blow off some stress through sex, and Shane had seemed as willing as usual.

Now, not even half an hour later, I sat in a chair by the bed, staring at his dead body, and heaved a sigh.

The door to the hotel room opened and soft footfalls approached.

"What happened?"

Rubbing the headache from my temples, I looked up at Eva. The woman was nearly six feet of lean killing intent. I'd be afraid of her if she wasn't one of my bodyguards.

Even so, I was still a little afraid of her.

I nodded at the body on the bed. "He tried to kill me."

We hadn't even finished getting undressed when I caught the flash of a needle. He'd tried to inject me with something, most likely poison, while I'd been in a seemingly vulnerable position. I had reacted on instinct and snapped his neck before the needle ever made contact with my skin.

Eva took a brief glance at the rapidly cooling corpse, then focused most of her attention on the syringe he'd tried to stick in me.

"Assassin?"

I sighed again and closed my eyes,

letting my head rest against the back of the chair. "Either this was his intent from the beginning, or someone found out he was my lover and turned him against me. Either way, same outcome."

Pulling out a small plastic container from her pocket, Eva safely stored the syringe so it could be tested later. "This is the third time this month someone has tried to kill you."

I grinned at her as I heard the door open again. "So, business as usual."

A man stepped up next to Eva, and I turned my smile on him instead.

"So, does our little assassin have any friends?"

Gavriil, Eva's partner and fellow bodyguard, scowled and shook his head. "The area seems clear. Your lover seemed to be working alone. Shall I prepare the usual removal?"

Eva and Gavriil had been my bodyguards for a long time. They were originally a gift from my distant Russian relatives when I took over as the head of the Bianchi family at only eighteen years old. After twenty years together, I rarely needed to give them orders anymore. They moved as fluidly around me as a pair of shadows.

Yet, as I looked over at the body in my bed, a new idea occurred to me.

"No. Shane was a good lover while we were together. It would be rude to simply throw away such a thoughtful gift. We should return it to its sender."

In all the years I'd known them, I could count on one hand the number of times I saw Eva or Gavriil laugh. On the outside they were as stoic and unmovable as a brick wall. Yet, our close acquaintance meant that I could read them better than the average person. Humor danced silently in their eyes. Although they said nothing but a simple acknowledgement of my order, I knew they wholeheartedly agreed with my decision.

A half hour later found me sitting in the back of my private car, with Gavriil behind the wheel, and Eva riding shotgun. Shane's body would be dealt with according to my orders, and a clean up crew had already been called to sanitize the hotel room. I wasn't worried about anyone reporting me. I owned the hotel, and my staff knew how to keep their heads down and not ask questions. However, as the head of one of the most powerful families of the Italian Mafia, it never hurt to be cautious.

It was the middle of the day, and New York was as busy as usual. The sun was high in the sky, and the streets were full of people. Our car crawled at a snail's pace. All the money and power in the world was still helpless against inner city traffic.

I tried not to show it, but I was in a bad mood. I'd gotten no sleep the night before due to overseeing the arrival of the new shipment, and I'd been hoping to at least work off some stress in bed. Instead, I was just as tired as before, with the added bonus of unsatisfied arousal simmering under my skin.

Why couldn't Shane have waited until after we had sex one more time before he tried to kill me?

Exhausted and horny was a terrible combination.

Traffic finally thinned out when we left the borders of the city and we flew down the highway at a much faster speed. It was only then, as I watched the familiar landscape pass by, that I realized I had no idea where we were going.

"Baltimore," Eva said when I asked.

"Baltimore?" I would never be so unsophisticated as to openly gape at her, but it was close. "Why are we going there? I have no business in Baltimore."

"You have a meeting there tonight, and it'll take over three hours to travel by car, so we need to leave now."

"Tell them to reschedule. I haven't slept in nearly forty hours. I'm not going to Baltimore tonight."

She turned in the front seat just enough to look into the back of the car. Her blue eyes, even paler than my own, laughed at me.

"The head of the Mariano family requested this meeting."

I sat up straighter in my seat. "Never mind. Keep driving."

Alex Mariano?

What did the newly christened leader of the whole Italian Mafia want to talk about?

There'd been some drama when Alex first took over for his father, which I had helped with, but surely that was all over now. Last I heard, Alex had been settling in well as he took over his father's affairs.

So, what was he doing in Baltimore?

The Mariano family had their finger in

nearly every pie possible, but as far as I knew, nothing important was happening in Baltimore right now.

Fuck, I was tired.

Whatever Alex needed to talk about was likely not going to be resolved quickly.

It was days like this that I was glad I'd paid extra for a car with reclining back seats. Leaning my seat back as far as it would go, I pulled off my jacket and draped it over my face to block out the sunlight.

"Wake me when we get there."

CHAPTER TWO

Oliver

MY DAY STARTED, like most days, with the smell of smoke in my nose and the flickering light of flames in my eyes. I'd once again dreamed about the day our family house burned down, and the heat still seemed trapped within the scar tissue on my face, despite being nearly fifteen years in the past.

Shaking off the nightmare, I rose for the day and started getting ready. My shift at the coffee shop started early, and the house was blissfully silent at six in the morning. Sitting at the kitchen table by myself, I idly drew a few ideas in my sketchbook with one hand while feeding myself toast with the other. Breakfast was the only time I had to myself, and while I hated waking up so early, I appreciated the silence.

It never lasted for long.

"Shouldn't you be leaving?" my grandmother said when she eventually emerged from her own bedroom. Technically, the whole house belonged to her. My mother, brother, and I just lived there. However, her old legs could no longer manage the stairs, so we lived upstairs while she stayed on the main floor.

If I didn't need to use the kitchen, I could have avoided her entirely.

As soon as the thought entered my mind, I chased it away. I should be grateful. She let us live in her house rent free. Without that generosity, there was no telling where we would have ended up.

"I'm leaving soon, Nana," I said as I packed my bag for the day. My sketchbook joined my barista uniform in the vain hope that I'd be able to draw more on my break.

It never happened, but I continued to remain optimistic.

As I was heading out the door, a car pulled up in front of the house. The woman who stepped out waved cheerfully at me before opening the back seat to collect her supplies.

I waved back, keeping a neutral expression on my face even as my grandmother stepped up beside me.

"Waste of money."

I sighed. "Nana." We had the same conversation every morning and never got anywhere. "The nurse needs to be here to help take care of Rowan. Mom has to work, and you can't manage his care on your own."

Standing on the front porch of the house, my gaze drifted up to the bedroom window where I knew my brother slept.

Rowan was only fifteen and had been born with Spinal Muscular Atrophy. It weakened his muscles to the point that he needed round the clock care. He put on a brave face, never complaining about his situation, but I knew how much his condition pained him, both emotionally and physically.

My bedroom sat right next to his, and some nights I heard him crying through the walls.

Nana just sniffed in disdain. "Your mother wouldn't need to waste her money on an at home nurse if you stayed here to take care of him instead of going off to that coffee job. Your salary doesn't even cover the cost of the nurse. It's a waste."

"Mother, stop giving Oliver a hard time," my own mother interrupted us as she also stepped out onto the porch. "He deserves to have his own life and not be trapped in the house all the time. Besides, an employment gap on his resume could make it harder for him to find work in the future. It's good that he's maintaining a job now.

I gave my mother a grateful smile but couldn't look at her for long. Heavy bags hung under her eyes, blatantly displaying her exhaustion to the world. She was a nurse and worked long hours at the nearby hospital. It helped us keep expenses down, since she could look after Rowan when she wasn't on shift, but the job ran her ragged.

I couldn't remember the last time my mother didn't look exhausted.

"I need to get going."

With a strained smile on her face, my mother wished me a good day before greeting the at home nurse who was walking up the porch steps.

I left before Nana could say anything else. The bus stop was only a few blocks away, so I didn't have far to walk. I'd been working at the same cafe since I turned eighteen. Four years of practice allowed me to time the commute perfectly. I arrived just as the bus I needed pulled up, so I didn't have to wait around.

It was early. The sun had barely made an appearance over the horizon, and a few lingering stars could still be seen in the sky. At such an hour, the bus wasn't packed yet, so I easily found a seat at the back where I wouldn't be disturbed.

From there, I had exactly thirty-two minutes before the bus reached my stop near the coffee shop. So, like I did most mornings, I pulled out my sketchbook. Except, this time I didn't draw. Instead, I opened a folder that I kept hidden at the back of the book.

Since my mother was so busy, I volunteered to help the household by managing our finances. It had started when I was sixteen, and my mother accidentally forgot to pay the bills one too many times. She nearly went to jail, though luckily she managed to avoid such a fate. Between her job and my brother, she just didn't have the energy to keep track of anything else, so I'd started managing the books for her.

Looking down at the numbers listed on the spreadsheet in my lap, I was once again thankful that I'd taken on the responsibility when I did. My mother didn't need a daily reminder of how hopeless our situation really was.

There was no sugarcoating it. We were screwed.

When Rowan had been born with SMA, the initial treatments had put us into a lifetime of debt. Then, just a few months after his birth, a house fire had stolen our home. The insurance payout had barely covered my burn treatment, and certainly wasn't going to buy us a new house. So we'd moved in with Nana.

Since then, Rowan's condition had improved enough to have a mostly normal lifespan, but SMA was genetic and progressive. It would never go away, and he would need continued treatment the rest of his life. Despite working so hard to pay for everything, it seemed like the financial hole we'd found ourselves in was just as deep as ever.

At the rate we were going, three lifetimes wouldn't be enough to pay off our debt. It was a hole we could never escape, unless we did something drastic.

Some days, the drastic option didn't seem so bad.

By the end of the bus ride, I'd managed to pay off a few bills through the banking app on my phone, and recalculated this week's budget. Rowan only needed treatment every few months, now, instead of every few weeks like when he was a baby, so there was a little more breathing room in between. His next treatment was coming up soon, and I needed to scrape together as much extra money as possible in the meantime to prepare for the inevitable expense.

CHAPTER THREE

D'Angelo

THE THREE HOURS to Baltimore seemed to pass in the space between breaths. It felt like I had just closed my eyes when Eva was nudging me awake and claiming that our destination was only a few minutes down the road.

I'd never spent much time in Baltimore before, but major cities all tended to look very similar at the heart. Tall buildings rose on either side of the street, blocking the view of the sky. The sun had set, and it was night now, but one could hardly tell due to the numerous streetlights and glowing advertisements hanging above every shop and restaurant.

The neon image of a cup of coffee caught my attention, and I ordered Gavriil to pull over. Three hours of sleep had barely scratched the surface of my exhaustion. In order to get through this meeting, I needed some caffeine in my veins.

Stepping through the front door of the cafe, I was surprised to find it empty. Sure, Baltimore wasn't as busy as a place like New York City, but it was still a major metropolitan. A cafe sitting in a prime spot on a main street should have been overflowing with customers.

I checked my watch. The time was later than I thought, and the shop closed in exactly three minutes.

While I hated to be that customer who came in right at the end of the day, I didn't have many other options. At this point coffee was a need, not just a want, and I was already in the shop. Backing out now would just be awkward.

No one stood behind the counter—which was understandable as they were probably in the back cleaning up for the night—so I was forced to ring the service bell. The high-pitched chime made me wince.

"Hold on just a moment, I'm coming," someone called from the back.

A young man shouldered his way through the swinging door, his hands laden with a large tray of freshly washed mugs and cutlery. His eyes were downcast, focusing on keeping the tray balanced, so I had a moment to observe him unnoticed. Fair, with tousled chestnut hair that hung longer in the front than in the back. Since he was turned to the side, I could only see him in profile, but he had a heart-shaped face with a small straight nose and just enough pronunciation in his cheekbones to give his face some definition without losing its natural softness.

All in all, just my type. Even his height was perfect. He stood on the shorter side of average. If I held him, his head would tuck comfortably under my chin.

From the side, I could just barely read the nametag on his uniform.

Oliver.

It was a fitting name. After such a hectic day, and the loss of my previous lover, it felt like the universe was offering me an olive branch by at least giving me something nice to look at.

"Sorry for the wait," Oliver said when he finally finished setting the mugs and silverware back in their place and turned toward me. "We're getting ready to close so I can't... oh."

Large hazel eyes stared at me, flickering down for a moment over the rest of my body before he seemed to realize what he was doing and quickly focused back on my face.

"I... sorry, I can't offer you much."

I knew I cut a striking figure. It wasn't a matter of arrogance. A lot of effort was put into my appearance for that very purpose. In my position, making an impact the moment I entered a room was half the battle, and had saved my life on more than one occasion.

Tipping my head in just a little to the side, I let my face settle into a charming smirk that almost always earned me a partner for the night.

"Good thing I'm not picky. What's the strongest thing you have available?"

"Um... the strongest?" He looked down at the counter, as if searching for something he couldn't find. A light blush dusted his cheeks.

It was only then that I noticed the man's most prominent feature that I'd somehow entirely overlooked. A large burn scar covered most of the left side of his face, all the way from hairline to jaw. The only excuse I could give was that his bright eyes were particularly distracting. Plus, the way his hair hung longer in the front and was parted more to one side did a spectacularly good job at hiding the scar.

It looked old. More silver than pink, signaling that the skin had healed a long time ago and the scar had settled into place. Still, based on its size, the burn must have been traumatic. It was a wonder that his eye hadn't been damaged.

He seemed to realize the moment my gaze settled on his scar, for he automatically turned just enough to the side so that I was mostly looking at the right side of his face. It was such an automatic move, like he hadn't even thought about it. He was obviously used to always presenting his "good" side to people.

"You'll have to be more specific. I'm not sure what you want."

My smile almost dropped.

What I wanted should be obvious.

Right, this conversation was about *coffee*. I'd almost forgotten my initial purpose for stepping into the cafe.

Still, there was no reason for flirting and coffee to be mutually exclusive. I could have both.

I leaned my hip against the counter, purposely angling myself so I could see more of the left side of his face. Scars weren't a turn off for me, and I wanted him to know it.

"Well, I want a lot of things." I trailed my gaze down his body, purposely lingering until I was certain he'd noticed. "However, for now, I'm looking for whatever drink you can offer that'll give me the most caffeine in one cup."

"Ah." His eyes lit up, making the hazel color practically sparkle. "The nurse's special."

"What?"

The blush returned to his cheeks, though he didn't look as shy as before. "Oh, there's a pretty big hospital nearby. A lot of nurses come here on their breaks, and they're often looking for something to help them get through their long shifts. So, we came up with a recipe just for them. It's basically, like a maxed-out espresso. Would that work?"

"Sounds perfect."

"Great."

He grabbed one of the neatly stacked to-go cups and turned to the elaborate coffee machine at the far side of the counter.

"You got here just in time. I was about to clean out the machine and shut everything down."

"Yeah." I leaned a little farther over the counter so I could watch him work. "Lucky me."

His hands were long and delicate, and moved with perfect precision. I'd bet my entire fortune that the man was an artist. It was too easy to picture him holding a paintbrush, creating masterpieces with a mere stroke of his fingers.

It was also easy to picture other things his hands could do for me, but I kept those thoughts to myself.

For now.

He also wore a surprising amount of jewelry. There were several rings on his fingers, along with multiple necklaces of varying lengths. However, what caught my eye was the ear cuff. It looked like a golden snake curling around the shell of his ear like it was whispering secrets to him, and a small apple charm hung from his earlobe.

The young man presented a charming portrait of contradictions. He was not only an olive branch of peace, but also a creature of wicked temptation.

If I didn't have such an important meeting lined up, I would definitely try to coax this man into my bed. Whatever Alex needed from me had better be important.

The drink took a few minutes to complete, and I noticed him doing something complicated with the milk pitcher. I wasn't complaining, since it gave me more time to watch him, but I was pleasantly surprised by the final result. A tall cup of rich coffee was carefully placed before me, filled all the way to the brim. The lid still sat beside the cup, showing off the artwork that had been created on the drink's surface.

I'd seen plenty of latte art before, but this was much more than the fancy heart or leaf that most barista's could do. This was very clearly a phoenix. I could even see the individual feathers, and the flames that rose up from its wings.

Taking out my phone, I snapped a picture of the drink. "Impressive. I knew you were an artist." I hated covering up the art, but I needed to put the lid on the cup in order to take it with me. The phoenix would just have to be content with living immortalized on my phone.

"Y-you knew? How?"

I handed over my credit card, and although Oliver was distracted staring at me in awe and confusion, he still managed to slide the card through the cash register without fumbling.

"You've got the look of an artist." When he handed the card back, I let our fingers brush. "Plus, you're obviously good with your hands."

With one finger, he nervously twirled a lock of his wavy hair. It was a cute gesture, but also allowed him to discreetly block my view of the scar on his face.

If I did take this man to bed, I'd tie up his hands so he couldn't hide from me.

For a moment, I was half-tempted to push back my meeting with Alex. He owed me a favor after I helped him when he was kidnapped.

The sound of a throat clearing drew my attention. Eva stood in the door of the cafe, scowling at me as she tapped her watch.

My break was over. It was time to get back to business.

I stuffed some cash into the tip jar on the counter, not even paying attention to how much. "Thanks for this." I saluted Oliver with the cup. "Sorry for keeping you so long. I'll let you finish closing up."

As I headed out the door, I heard the barista stutter over his words. "It's... uh, you're a pleasure."

I stopped just before the door could close behind me and looked back at him, one eyebrow raised in a silent question.

Realizing what he'd said, Oliver's face bloomed a bright crimson red. "I mean... you're welcome. It's my pleasure."

Taking a moment to sip my coffee, which was just as strong as promised, I regarded him from head to toe. "Hmm. Not yet, it's not. Ciao bella."

With that cryptic remark hanging in the air, I left without further explanation. It was entirely by design. I was certain the beautiful effeminate man would be turning my words over for a while, wondering what I meant and if my suggestive tone was intentional.

Good. I liked the idea of living in his brain long after I was gone.

As we headed back to the car, I could feel Eva giving me a judging look out of the corner of her eye.

"Something to say?" I asked before taking another sip of my coffee.

"You just killed your previous lover a few hours ago."

"Yes." I waited while Gavriil opened the car door for me. "Which means I am in need of another one. Maybe this one won't try to stab me in the neck with a syringe."

For a moment, she looked like she would argue, but something in my expression must have tipped her off that I wasn't in the mood, for she looked back at the cafe with a thoughtful expression.

"Maybe, depending on how the meeting with Mariano goes, we can come back."

For Eva, that was basically permission to fuck around as much as I wanted. Now I just needed to get through the meeting with Alex.

CHAPTER FOUR

Oliver

BUSINESS AT THE coffee shop was usually slow at first, no one wanted to be awake at such early hours, but picked up around eight when the morning commuters stopped in on their way to work. After four years, I could practically manage the front counter in my sleep. I had coworkers, of course, but most came and went so quickly that I barely bothered to learn their names. Everyone knew to just do whatever task I assigned them, and let me work on my own.

It wasn't a bad job, and it did give me opportunities to express my creative side.

Latte art was, perhaps, not the most refined medium, but it was fun, and it brought a smile to people's day. A warm feeling bloomed in my chest every time someone stopped to take a picture of their drink, knowing that my creation would live on in the digital world.

I was a few hours into my shift when I got my first unusual order. A rather nondescript man stepped up to the counter and said that they were there to pick up a to-go order that they'd already called in.

This wasn't unusual. Many people didn't want to wait and would place their order ahead of time with the shop's online app. However, when I checked the computer system, I noticed a green dot next to their name on the order.

Turning on the coffee press to start the man's order, I stepped into the back room and grabbed another to-go cup that was waiting in a locked cabinet. It was already labeled with the man's name.

This was why I kept the job despite the minimum wage salary not even covering the price of my brother's nurse. The owner of the shop also secretly sold marijuana on the side, and paid me extra under the table to handle the exchange.

The owner would prepare the "green" orders the night before, and I just had to look for the colored dot next to a customer's name. From there, all I had to do was grab their extra cup from the back, hand it over along with their legitimate order, and not ask any questions.

It was a good deal. For very little effort, I practically doubled my salary, making more than enough to cover Rowan's nurse, plus a little extra.

Of course, this deal only worked so long as the owner's weed business had to remain secret. The legalization of marijuana seemed inevitable in the near future. If that happened, the owner wouldn't need to pay me extra anymore, and I'd probably have to find a new job.

Or possibly give in to Nana's preferences and become my brother's full-time nurse.

I was scheduled to work a double shift, from opening to closing. Throughout the day, several more "green" orders came in, which I handled the same as the first one.

By the end of the day, when there was only a few minutes left before we closed, I breathed a sigh of relief. Nothing too bad had happened, other than the typical customer rudeness. I'd even managed to send the other staff home a few minutes early. The cafe was empty so late in the evening, and I could handle the last bit of cleanup.

It was three minutes until closing, and I was in the back room making sure the special cabinet was locked properly, when I heard the service bell on the front counter ring.

Great. One last customer. Hopefully, they just wanted something quick so I wouldn't have to stay too late past closing. It was Thursday, and I needed to get home as quickly as possible.

Grabbing a tray of clean mugs out of the wash, I brought them with me as I returned to the front counter, trying to finish my duties as soon as possible.

When I saw who waited for me on the other side of the counter, my irritation over the last-minute customer vanished.

He was tall, with dark olive toned skin and a full head of thick, dark hair. The black-on-black suit he wore was almost completely colorless, except for a pale blue pocket square that perfectly matched his eyes.

I would have said that he looked neatly put together, except for the tension around his eyes and unshaved stubble on his chin that indicated he'd had a long day. Most people who came to the coffee shop were tired in one way or another, so I was familiar with the look of someone who hadn't slept in a while. Yet, this man somehow managed to wear his exhaustion like a fashion choice. It gave a rough edge to his otherwise refined appearance, like an elegant knife that was unexpectedly serrated on one side.

It had been a while since I found myself blushing over a man. Usually, I didn't have the opportunity. Most people took one look at the scar covering the left side of my face and immediately averted their eyes. It made me feel contagious, like they thought my disfiguration would spread to them if they stared too long.

My typical defense was to dial my smile up to eleven and kill them with kindness. However, this time, that defense wouldn't work. The man didn't shy away from looking at my scars, and even seemed to be flirting with me.

When he spoke, there was a slight

accent to his words. I couldn't immediately place it, other than just a vague sense of *foreign*. His English was perfectly fluent, but I suspected he wasn't originally born in an English speaking country. Perhaps somewhere Mediterranean, based on his skin tone, but the blue eyes threw me for a loop. Either way, it was way too easy to picture him on a beachside villa, dressed in nothing but the smallest swimsuit as he soaked up the sunlight.

I swallowed past the knot that had formed in my throat. My smile felt awkward on my face. There was no instruction manual for how to handle these kinds of situations, and I was severely out of practice. I'd flirted with people before, of course. Even participated in a few heavy make out sessions, but it had always felt like more of an obligation than actual attraction. Like I was just going through the motions because that was what I was supposed to do. The situation with my family always kept me so busy, I didn't have time to think about anything else, and for a while, I'd even entertained the idea that I was asexual.

Well, that idea was now tossed right out the window. I was definitely attracted to the man. In fact, if I kept staring at him any longer, I was going to end up with a problem that would be hard to hide.

Quickly turning away from him, I started working on his order while silently begging my hormones to give me a break.

The man watched me as I worked. He wasn't even trying to hide his hungry gaze.

I shivered.

Being stared at could be just as bad as being avoided. Some people were weirdly fascinated by my scars and treated them like an invitation to gawk at me like I was a zoo exhibit.

Yet, this man's stare didn't feel like that, either. If anything, he made me feel like a work of art, and he was trying to memorize every detail.

It took everything I had not to drop the cup when I finally handed it over.

"Impressive," the man said when he looked at the cup.

I didn't even remember making the artwork on top of the drink. My hands had moved automatically, bringing to life whatever image was in my head. I was just as surprised as he was when I looked down at the design. A phoenix. Of course. Whenever my mind was left to wander, my thoughts always returned to fire.

The man smiled. "I knew you were an artist."

How had he known that?

I hadn't said anything about it.

Had I?

Since first laying eyes on the man, I barely noticed the words that had spilled out of my mouth. Surely, I wouldn't have wasted his time by blabbering on about my useless hobby.

When I asked him how he knew, the man made an obviously flirtatious comment about my hands.

Yes, the man was flirting. I wasn't reading too much into it.

The only question was, why?

He couldn't actually mean it. Even without my scared face as a deterrent, a man like this would not be interested in me. I was a poor little nobody up to my eyes in debt, and this man radiated power and money. His suit fit him too perfectly. This was not an outfit that he just pulled off the rack. It was obviously designer, and definitely bespoke. He didn't wear much jewelry, but the few pieces he did wear made a statement. His watch, alone, could probably pay my over the table salary for half a year.

No. A man like this would not be interested in me. He was probably just bored and decided to entertain himself by making me hot under the collar.

So, distracted by my racing thoughts, I tripped over my words and ended up mashing two phrases together in the worst way possible.

"Uh, I mean..." I stuttered as he looked at me with one curious eyebrow cocked at a deadly angle. "You're welcome. It's my pleasure."

There. That was two full sentences I'd managed to say without messing anything up. I wasn't a complete embarrassment.

His eyes practically glowed with inner heat as he looked me up and down. "Not yet, it's not."

Then, with a few casual Italian words tossed in amongst his English, he disappeared out the door.

Not yet?

What was that supposed to mean?

Did it actually mean anything, or was he just being cryptic for the sake of it?

I stood behind the counter, dazed and confused from the whirlwind interaction, until my phone alarm shocked me back into action.

Fuck.

If I didn't hurry, I was going to miss my bus.

Rushing through the rest of the clean up, I ran down the street after locking the door behind me.

I could not afford to be late. Not today.

CHAPTER FIVE

D'Angelo

OUR DESTINATION TURNED out to be the backroom of a nearby club. The Mariano family owned various properties in nearly every major city along the east coast, including many clubs, so this wasn't a surprise. Nightclubs weren't my favorite place, and even I owned a few. They were just too convenient. A lot of money could be pushed through them, and the constant stream of people coming and going easily hid nearly any type of activity.

Upon opening the door to the backroom, I was greeted to the sight of

Alex Mariano straddling the lap of his bodyguard and grinding like he was on the dance floor.

"Please tell me this isn't what you called me here for," I said to get the pair's attention. "I have plenty of kinks, but voyeurism isn't one of them."

Alex looked up from the deep kiss he'd been sharing with his bodyguard, but the brat didn't even look embarrassed as he smiled at me.

"You took too long. I got bored."

Swallowing the last dregs of my coffee, I tossed the cup in a nearby trashcan and sat in one of the room's other chairs. "I have a busy schedule, and I was up in New York when you contacted me. You're lucky I got here as quickly as I did. Why are we here, anyway? The Mariano family doesn't have much business in Baltimore."

The bodyguard, Garrison, moved off the chair so Alex could sit properly and face me. Although he'd only been with Alex for less than a year, he seemed just as efficient as my own bodyguards, standing just behind the person he meant to protect. For someone so new to the mafia lifestyle, he fit in surprisingly well, probably due to his extensive career in the Special Forces. Between him and Alex, who had spent his entire life training to one day take over as head of the Italian Mafia, they were not enemies that I wanted to fight.

Although, Alex's non-threatening act was very convincing. He pouted up at Garrison, as if cared about nothing but continuing their previous activities. If I didn't know better, I'd think he really was just the harmless brat that he pretended to be.

A moment later, when Garrison just scowled at him and gave him a look that clearly told him to focus, Alex's harmless mask slipped away. Dark eyes sharpened, and he relaxed back in his chair with the grace of a predator. His claws were sheathed for now, but they could come out at any time if necessary.

"It turns out my father's affairs are not so easily addressed. He left a lot of loose ends when he died." As he spoke, Alex rested his chin on his hand. The scars on his knuckles stood out starkly against his Mediterranean complexion. "Apparently, he made a deal with the Russians that I am now on the hook for."

Something bristled in Alex's eyes that immediately had me on guard. The man was not happy, and that did not bode well for whatever he needed from me.

"On the hook?" I repeated. "That doesn't sound good. What happened?"

Alex sighed but didn't immediately explain.

I understood his hesitance. Whatever trouble he'd found likely put him in a bad position. He was already so new to his leadership, and disadvantage could be disastrous for him. Although we were both part of the Italian Mafia, as the leader of the Bianchi family, I was also technically a rival. If he lost power, I could use it as an opportunity to gain that power for myself.

Lucky for him, I had no desire to do so. I was comfortable with my place in the world. I didn't need to change it. Only maintain it.

I softened my tone and my expression, leaning forward in my chair to try and emphasize my sincerity. "Alex. You obviously wanted to meet with me because you think I can help, but that'll only work if you tell me everything that's going on. Otherwise I can't help you, and you're just wasting both of our time."

He sighed, and Garrison put a hand on his shoulder to comfort him. It was a vulnerable show of emotion, revealing that the relationship between these two was more than just physical.

I considered it a compliment that they trusted me not to use their relationship against them. There were plenty of others who would, but I vowed to keep it to myself. The pair were cute, and obviously worked well together.

Patting Garrison's hand, Alex sat up straight, and the steel returned to his eyes.

"Apparently, my father made a deal with the Pahkan. A fairly standard drugs for guns deal."

The Pahkan, the leader of the Russian Mafia, rarely handled deals himself. Usually one of his four Brigadiers would handle these kinds of negotiations. For the Pahkan himself to be involved it must have either been a much larger deal than Alex was making it sound, or there was something else going on behind the scenes on the Russian end of things.

"Okay." I nodded, refusing to admit that this was all new information to me.

Usually, I was well informed about the movements of the Russian Mafia. This deal must have been kept under particularly tight wraps if my information networks didn't pick it up.

"So far, I'm not seeing a problem, or anything I can help with."

Alex's lip twitched, like he wanted to snarl. "The problem is that the Pahkan held up the Russian end of the deal while my father didn't. I don't know why he didn't. It's not like we couldn't afford it. Meanwhile, the Russians won't even talk to me other than to accuse me of helping my father break the deal with them. The whole thing is a mess, and if this continues, I'm afraid we might be heading toward war. I'm sure I don't have to tell you that a war between us and the Russians would be very bad for everyone."

No, he didn't need to tell me. I was acutely aware of how bad a war between the Italian and Russian Mafia would be.

If such a thing happened, I would suffer more than anyone.

Avoiding war between the Italian and Russian families was the very reason I existed in the first place. My father was the previous head of the Bianchi family.

However, my mother was a distant cousin of the Pahkan. Their marriage had been arranged as a sort of peace treaty between the two organizations.

My mixed blood is what gave me power in the criminal underworld since I was connected to so many influential people. However, if war broke out between Italian and Russian families, my mixed heritage could also be my undoing. My whole empire, which I worked hard to maintain, would be torn in half.

None of these racing thoughts showed on my face as I stared at Alex across the few feet of air that divided us. "And you want me to..."

"Mediate," Alex said with an exhausted edge to his voice. "Convince the Russians to communicate with me. Help me figure out what I need to do or give them to avoid this war. Mentioning your name was the only way I got them to speak with me at all. They're going to be sending someone to meet with me here in Baltimore, and I need you there at the meeting to help smooth things over."

Taking a deep breath through my nose, I forced my pulse to slow down. So far it seemed like a salvageable situation.

It wasn't even that complicated. A broken deal could be fixed.

There was just one detail in Alex's entire explanation that confused me.

"Why Baltimore?"

As far as I knew, the Russian Mafia had no special connection to this city.

Alex waved one hand in the air like he was batting away an annoying fly. "I have no idea. They wouldn't tell me why it had to be here. Just gave me a time and a place to show up. The whole thing smells like a trap, but not showing up isn't really a choice at the moment."

My first instinct was to immediately agree to help Alex. Out of everyone in the room, I had the most to lose, and I wanted it settled as quickly as possible.

It was precisely because I had the most to lose, however, that I had to be cautious.

"Alex," I said, keeping my voice soft. "I want to help you, but you must realize how risky it is for me to get involved. If things go badly..."

I didn't need to finish my statement. Everyone in the room knew what was at stake.

Alex nodded. "I know, but I need your

help with this. However, I don't expect your assistance for free. I'm here to make a deal with you."

My interest was piqued. Since Alex knew how risky this situation was for me, he must have come armed with something valuable to tempt me.

"What kind of deal?" I asked, trying not to sound too eager.

Alex smirked. He knew he had my attention.

"Recently, you've been interested in branching out from dealing recreational drugs to medical ones. If you help me settle things with the Russians, I'll bankroll that new project."

When the head of the Mariano family came fishing for assistance, he certainly knew what bait to use.

The distribution of medical drugs had been a pet project of mine for years. For generations, my family had focused on dealing recreational drugs. Cocaine, heroin, meth, etc...

However, there were even more people in this country who needed regular access to medical drugs. It wasn't just a matter of addiction. They needed these medications to stay alive. In other countries, where health care was free and medication was cheap, it wasn't a problem. However, in America, many necessary medical drugs were very expensive.

If we could offer those same drugs at a cheaper price, we could make a fortune. Plus, unlike recreational drugs, medical drugs actually helped keep customers alive, so they could keep being customers and keep paying us.

There was plenty of potential if I could get it set up. Unfortunately, there wasn't a lot of infrastructure for dealing in medical drugs. The big drug companies were determined to keep a hold of their monopoly, and finding a way to undermine them would require a big initial investment. I could technically afford it, but it would require draining my resources much more than I was comfortable with.

If Alex footed the upfront cost, however, I could probably get the whole operation up and running in a couple of years.

As I thought everything over for a few minutes, out of the corner of my eye, I noticed Alex grinning at me. He knew he had me. I could pretend to mull the offer over as long as I wanted, but at the end of the day, I was going to agree to his deal. There was too much at stake for me to turn him down.

I glanced toward Eva and Gavriil. They also knew what my answer would be, and I could practically see the wheels turning in their heads as they made the necessary plans. First on the list would be to acquire a temporary residence in Baltimore. Negotiations with the Russian Mafia would not move quickly, and if they were insisting on meeting in Baltimore, then it looked like I would be calling this city home for a while as well.

CHAPTER SIX

Oliver

I MANAGED TO catch the bus with only seconds to spare, slipping through the doors right before they closed. It had been a long day and I was tired, but I did not dare close my eyes. If I did, I might fall asleep and miss my stop, and I needed to get home as quickly as possible.

Some deity must have been smiling at me, because the bus actually managed to run on time for once. It dropped me off at the stop near my house, and I ran until the familiar front porch was in sight.

"Hey, Oliver," Rowan's voice greeted me as soon as I stepped through the door.

With one foot already on the stairs to the second floor, I froze in shock, then turned around. "Hey, Rowan. Having a good day today?"

My fifteen-year-old brother sat in his wheelchair in front of the living room television, watching Wheel of Fortune with Nana. His grin could have replaced the sun.

"Yep. I managed to walk down the stairs all on my own."

Spinal Muscular Atrophy created a weakness in muscles and ligaments. To put it simply, his body just couldn't support itself, and even simple movements were often difficult. Some days it was a struggle for him to even sit up unassisted. To actually walk down the stairs on his own must mean he was having a very good day.

I wasn't fooled into thinking this would be a permanent improvement. Good days came, and good days left. Tomorrow, he could be bedridden again, but for now I was just happy that he was happy.

"That's great, bud. I'm glad you had a good day. Do you and mom have anything special planned for tonight?"

"Mom's making garlic bread," Rowan

practically cheered, like it was the best news ever. "And there's a marathon of Godzilla movies running all night."

"Sounds like you guys have it all planned out."

I saw the frown on Nana's face and knew she had something to say, so I darted into the kitchen before she could utter a single word.

"Hey, mom. Rowan says there's garlic bread?"

From her position at the kitchen counter stirring a pot of spaghetti, she nodded toward the oven. "It's still baking, but it should be done by now. Could you check on it?"

"Sure thing."

Just as she said, the homemade garlic bread was perfectly golden. I pulled it out of the oven and immediately grabbed a piece to take a bite. It burned the roof of my mouth, so I quickly sucked in air to cool it down while still eating.

"Slow down, it's not going anywhere," my mother chided me.

"Sorry, mom. I'm just in a rush. I promised Ashes I'd be over soon."

"All right."

I could hear the sad tone in her voice,

though she didn't try to argue with me. She never did. The few times she'd raised her voice at me, her gaze drifted toward the left side of my face, and she fell silent.

I hated the sadness and guilt that constantly hung over her like a dark cloud. Every time I saw it made me feel like I'd drunk pure acid and my stomach rolled unpleasantly. Because of this, I usually kept our interactions short.

Heading upstairs, I dropped off my work stuff in my room and grabbed another already packed bag. My sketchbook never left my side since I didn't want anyone stumbling across the folder of financial information hidden in the back, so I took a moment to transfer it to my new bag. Then, after splashing some water on my face to try and wash off the exhaustion, I headed for the door.

Nana was waiting for me. On the surface, it looked like she was giving me some more garlic bread to take with me, but I knew she really just wanted an excuse to lecture me.

"Are you really going out again? You do this every night your mother has off work. Stay and spend some time with your family for once. Rowan is having a good day and he wants to watch these giant lizard movies with you."

I took the garlic bread she offered me but didn't look her in the eye. "Sorry, Nana. Maybe next time. I've... um, I've already made plans."

"Yes, yes." She waved me off. "Go spend time with your friend. Obviously, that's more important than your family."

"Oh, come on, Nana," I said, even as I reached for the door. "You know nothing is more important than family."

The door had almost closed behind me when I caught the faint sound of her voice.

"You say that, but you certainly don't show it."

Biting the inside of my cheek, I closed the door softly, so the latch barely made a sound. I stood on the porch for a moment, watching my shadow change shape under the flickering porch light. Hot tears stung my eyes. On my right side the tear fell easily, but on my left it got lost in the creases of my scars.

I wiped both away with the back of my hand and took a deep breath.

Now wasn't the time to get emotional. If I didn't hurry, I was going to be late.

Running down the road back toward the bus stop, I pulled out my phone and selected one of my few saved contacts.

"Hey, Oliver," Ashes' familiar voice greeted me.

"Hey, Ashes. You still good to cover for me tonight?"

"Yep. If your family asks, you were with me all night."

"Thanks again. You're the best."

"You know it. Stay safe. Call me in the morning."

The phone disconnected with a beep just as my bus arrived. I got on, but there weren't any seats open. So, I leaned against a pole and tried to catch my breath as the bus started heading in the opposite direction from Ashes' place.

My friend's full name was Ashley Sanger, but no one called them that. They preferred the gender-neutral adaptation of their name, Ashes.

I'd met Ashes shortly after the fire, and we'd been best friends ever since. I supported them when they came out as non-binary and helped them find a place to live when their family kicked them out. Because of this, Ashes' loyalty was unwavering. When I asked them to lie for me, they did, without question.

I hated using my friend as a cover story, but I didn't have much choice. My family would never let me leave the house again if they knew where I was going.

Most nights, when I came home from the coffee house, I took care of my brother so the at home nurse could leave. However, my mother didn't work on Thursday and Friday nights, so I was free to do whatever I wanted without fear of leaving Rowan helpless.

If given the choice, I would have much rather stayed home.

Another half hour bus ride dropped me off in the center of downtown Baltimore, right outside a gay club called the *Erodance*. It was more upscale than your average strip club, but it still catered to desires of the flesh all the same.

I avoided the front door, and went in through the back like the rest of the employees.

When I was asked as a child what I wanted to be when I grew up, I always said the same thing. I wanted to be an artist. Well, in a way, I was. As an exotic dancer, I created art of a sort, although I used my body instead of a brush.

EVIE RILEY

The backstage area of the club was a chaotic mix of red velvet couches that were so old they were practically threadbare, and dozens of dressing tables lined up for the dancer's use. I found my usual table, off to the side where I preferred it, and started getting ready.

The first thing I put on was my mask. In the club, I was never seen without it. Even my fellow dancers barely knew what I looked like. It covered the left side of my face, which not only hid my scars, but also kept my identity a secret. I had several different masks to match the different outfits hanging on my personal clothing rack.

Well, the costumes barely counted as outfits. Really, they were just bits of fabric and string that seemed to be more glitter than substance. Technically, they covered what needed to be covered so I was not completely naked, but little was left to the imagination.

Because of the mask, I'd been given the stage name Phantom. As soon as I arrived, I checked the schedule to see what routines I'd be performing in, and which costumes would be needed.

Tonight, I was assigned to wear a

delicate silver creation that reminded me of something from a fairytale.

Everything at the club was fast-paced. There was barely twenty minutes between my arrival and my first performance.

As I approached the stage from the wings, I tuned out everything around me. I didn't see the club or the patrons waiting just past the curtain. I didn't even see my fellow dancers. There was just me, and the silver pole on stage about a dozen feet away that I would be performing on.

The only thought in my head was the choreography.

And the fact that I was cold.

For a place where the employees walked around with ninety-five percent of their skin on display, one would think they could turn the heat up a little. I had goosebumps everywhere, and my nipples felt hard enough to cut diamonds.

Maybe that was the point.

There were a few performances before mine, which I watched with disinterested attention.

Genie in a Bottle.

She Wolf.

I Need a Hero.

The club was definitely having a

fantasy theme that night.

After each performance, I watched the back door on the other side of the stage. Each time, the performer disappeared through it, along with at least one of the club's patrons.

Unlike a typical strip club, guests did not throw money on stage. Each performer was given a standard paycheck, and they could leave it at that if they wanted.

However, the real money was made in the back. Guests could purchase a "private show" if they wanted, and the dancer agreed. They claimed it was just dancing, but everyone knew what really happened behind those doors.

Just the other night, I'd been offered twenty thousand dollars to give a guest a "private show". I'd turned them down. My body may be on display, but it wasn't for sale.

However, as I waited for my turn to perform, I couldn't help thinking of the secret folder at the back of my sketchbook. Even with my mom's job, my job, my under the table paycheck from the coffee house, and the money I made dancing, we were still barely making any headway.

Twenty thousand dollars wouldn't solve our debt problem, but it would definitely help. And if I kept giving "private shows", eventually, I might even be able to pay it all off. My family could finally be debt free. Rowan could be set up with even better care, and my mother wouldn't have to work so hard.

All it would cost would be... me.

If I gave my body away, then my family could finally thrive.

What was I even saving myself for anyway?

It wasn't like anyone actually wanted me. I was hanging on to something worthless when I could be profiting off it.

I had half a mind to find the manager for that night and tell them that I would accept any "private show" requests. However, an image of the man from earlier popped into my mind.

I didn't know his name, but he had definitely been flirting with me. I still didn't know what he saw that made him take an interest, even just a passing one, but it gave me hope that maybe I still had some value in the eyes of others.

The song for my performance started.

Putting on a sultry expression, I stepped out onto the stage under the spotlights and grabbed the pole to start my routine.

I wouldn't accept any "private shows" that night. I wasn't sure what I was waiting for, but I could afford to wait a little longer.

CHAPTER SEVEN

D'Angelo

IT WAS A week before I was able to go back to the coffee shop. Usually, once I'd set my sights on someone, I moved on them as quickly as possible. A week was probably longer than I'd ever waited before, but dealing with the Russians was proving more difficult than expected. Whatever Alex's father had done had really insulted them, because even getting any of the Pahkan's men to talk to me ended up being extremely difficult.

Finally, however, I managed to set up a meeting with a Russian representative so we could at least get the ball rolling. Only then was I able to return to the coffee shop, this time earlier in the day.

The sun shone through shop windows, glinting off the earring dangling off Oliver's ear when he looked up at the sound of the bell over the door. For a moment, a stiff customer service smile covered his face, but a complex mix of emotions immediately replaced it when he realized who he faced. Just like before, he instinctively turned himself slightly to the side, keeping his scars out of sight.

"Oh, um... hi. I mean... hello. *Welcome to Brew Crew Coffee.*"

Brew Crew Coffee?

Oh, right, the name of the coffee shop. I hadn't even bothered to check the name of the place. The shop itself held no value to me beyond the man behind the counter.

There were no other customers in the shop at that moment, so nothing stood in my way as I approached the counter. I watched Oliver fidget under my attention and tried not to let the heat show in my eyes as I imagined him writhing under my gaze for a different reason and in an entirely different situation.

"I have to say, you look even better in

the daylight.”

I expected the other man to blush and get embarrassed, or maybe even scoff and tell me to leave if he wasn't interested in me. What I didn't expect was laughter, but that's exactly what I got.

Oliver snickered behind his hand, biting his lip in a failed attempt at holding back the sound. Hazel eyes glittered brighter than his jewelry when he looked at me.

“That's the first thing you say to me? After a week? You certainly like to come on strong, don't you?”

The unexpected reaction was refreshing. My smile widened, and I held out both my hands to the sides as if putting myself on display.

“Of course. I'm a busy man, and I hate the way people so often dance around each other when they could just say what they mean. Besides...” I leaned forward until my hip braced against the counter. “I don't think you mind.”

The blush I'd expected earlier finally spread over his cheeks. For a moment, he seemed to forget about his scars and faced me directly. His posture relaxed, and I was already celebrating my victory, but his self-consciousness settled back onto his shoulders like an iron cloak.

Clearing his throat, he turned partially away and clawed at his bangs to make sure they covered the left side of his face.

"What, um... what makes you say that?"

At least he was still willing to engage with me. I hadn't lost yet.

"Well, you noticed how long I was gone." My smile softened until it was only the slightest curve of my lips, and I let some of the heat show in my eyes. "That means you've been thinking about me."

It was the moment of truth. I would know from his reaction if there was truly any interest behind those hazel eyes.

"I would never think inappropriately about a customer," Oliver said with a little extra breath in his voice. "Besides, I don't even know your name, sir."

"D'Angelo," I said, completely ignoring my last name. A regular civilian likely wouldn't recognize the significance of the Bianchi name, but there was always a chance, and I didn't feel like using any of my aliases.

Although, he did bring up a good point.

Technically, I was a customer. Usually, I picked up my partners from clubs, bars, or the various events I attended. Occasionally, I hooked up with the family or friends of my various connections who were already part of the criminal underground life that I lived in. This was my first time taking an interest in a service worker. Not that there was anything wrong with the job, but the employee-customer dynamic could cause problems.

Turning off the charm for a moment, I addressed Oliver with a serious tone. "Just to be clear, you can absolutely tell me to fuck off. My ego can take it, and I'm not interested in anything that isn't mutual."

Oliver nodded, though he didn't look as relieved as I'd hoped. "That's good to know..." He trailed off, and couldn't seem to decide between looking at my eyes or looking anywhere but my eyes. "However, I still don't really know you."

Oh, so he was the type who wanted to talk first. I was used to partners who immediately wanted to jump into bed, though that was probably at least partly due to the environment where I chose to meet potential lovers. However, I could work with this. It would mean a little more effort, but the outcome would be worth it.

How about this?" I laid my credit card on the counter. "Ring me up an espresso, and whatever drink you like best, then come share it with me and talk for a bit. That way we can get to know each other."

Oliver looked uncertainly around the shop. I could practically see the wheels turning in his head as he weighed the pros and cons of my offer. It had been the same the last time we talked, and I suspected that the man was a chronic overthinker.

"All right," he finally said, and started punching buttons on the cash register. "It's dead right now, so I have nothing to do, but if another customer comes in, I'll have to leave to take care of them."

I easily agreed to his requirements, safe in the knowledge that no one would disturb us. Gavriil and Eva had spent twenty minutes chasing away anyone who tried to come into the shop before I'd stepped inside and they would continue to do so until I left.

While Oliver was busy making the

drinks, I slipped a hundred dollar bill into the tip jar on the counter to make up for the loss of business.

Oliver was efficient at his job. I'd barely sat down at a table in the far corner, away from the windows and door, when he joined me carrying two drinks. The espresso came in a delicate cup, which he placed in front of me, while his own drink seemed to be something iced. I could hear the ice shifting around in the cup every time it moved and condensation dripped down the side of the glass.

Taking a sip of my coffee, I watched Oliver over the rim of my cup. He stared down at his drink without touching it, letting his hair fall partially over his face while nervously twirling one of the rings on his fingers.

For someone who had insisted on 'getting to know each other,' he didn't seem keen to talk.

Sighing quietly to myself, I set my cup down with a soft clink against the table. "That's interesting jewelry you're wearing."

He stopped toying with the ring and gave me a confused look.

"It's custom work," I continued,

pointing between the rings, necklace, and earrings that he wore. "And all made by the same artist, if I'm not mistaken. It's quality work."

The last time I saw him, all his jewelry was filled with Garden of Eden symbolism. Today, however, was a cosmic theme. Vastly different designs, yet there was a similarity in the construction that said it was all made by the same hand. To have so many pieces from the same artist, they must have some significance to him.

My instincts turned out to be right as Oliver lit up, his nervousness forgotten as he held out his hands to show off the rings he wore.

"My friend, Ashes, made it all. They're really good, and they've got a popular online business. I really wouldn't be able to afford any of this, but they usually give me the experimental pieces when they're trying out a new idea."

From there, conversation flowed much easier as Oliver started talking about how he'd known Ashes since elementary school and telling me stories from their shared childhood. I would have been jealous that Oliver was spending so much time talking about someone else, if it weren't for the clearly platonic, sibling-like relationship they seemed to have.

Plus, the conversation topic allowed me to pick up some crucial information about Oliver.

He'd had the scars on his face since he was very young. Money was very tight for his family due to his younger brother's genetic illness. And, most importantly, Oliver had a passion for art.

"There were free after school classes," he explained as he showed me some of the drawings in his sketchbook. "I didn't know it at the time, but my mom basically used it as daycare for me while she worked. The only thing I cared about was that the classes were fun. The art teacher was also great and would often let me stay late even after the free class was over. Since then, I've dabbled in all kinds of different mediums, although I think watercolors are my favorites. I'd love to get into oil painting, but oil-based paints are expensive, not to mention the cost of canvases and brushes. Watercolors I can just do on paper."

The pictures in the sketchbook were simple pencil drawings, obviously just a collection of random thoughts rather than finished pieces. There were several portraits, probably of people he knew, a cute dog that he'd passed on the street, and even a sunrise that he'd seen one morning on his way to work. Although the picture was in black and white, each stroke of the pencil was so finely placed that I could easily imagine the colors.

I turned the page again, revealing an unfinished image. It was another portrait, and although the figure's features were only partially defined, I still recognized myself.

Oliver quickly snapped the sketchbook closed. "Forget about that. It's, um... that was just... sorry."

Propping my elbows on the table, I let my chin rest atop my laced fingers. "I'm flattered. Does this mean you see me as a work of art?"

Oliver scowled at me, sticking out his lower lip in a way that begged me to bite it.

"They say fishing for compliments is a sign of insecurity."

My grin turned sharp and just a bit lecherous. "What do you say? Do you think I'm insecure?"

He honestly studied me for a moment

as if he was actually considering the possibility. "No," he eventually concluded. "You're spoiled and you like teasing other people too much."

I scoffed. "Spoiled? Hardly. I'll have you know, my parents only let me have two ponies growing up. All my friends had at least three."

Finishing off the last swallow of his drink, Oliver rolled his eyes at me. "I'm so sorry. I didn't realize your childhood was full of such suffering."

The sarcasm in his voice couldn't have been more obvious.

Worry flashed over his face for a moment, causing his scars to pull at the edges of healthy skin. He must have worried that he'd offended me. If I was actually as insecure as he implied, I would have been.

Luckily, I'd always had a very healthy ego, so I just laughed.

"In all honesty, you're probably right. I was a spoiled little brat. I threw a tantrum every time I lost at tag or hide-and-seek." Taking a risk, I reached out and grabbed Oliver's hand, letting my thumb press against the pulse point of his wrist. "That hasn't really changed. I still prefer to get my way. I've just moved on to more adult games."

Under my thumb, I felt Oliver's pulse flutter. His breath became shallow and uneven, and he stared down at our joined hands like he didn't quite know what he was looking at.

Then, unexpectedly, his brow furrowed, and he grabbed my wrist to bring my watch closer to his face. "Crap. Is that really the time?" He stood up so quickly that his chair toppled over, and he scanned the store. "I can't believe you let me ramble on so long. Thank God no one came in. Usually, we're super busy this time of day."

No one would be coming in so long as Gavriil and Eva were guarding the place, but Oliver didn't need to know that. Instead, I just grabbed his hand again, forcing him to look at me.

"Don't say that. I like listening to you talk. I definitely want to hear more. Let me take you to dinner. What time do you get off work?"

After such a pleasant conversation, I thought I had the other man locked down. Yet, to my surprise, Oliver suddenly turned shifty and pulled away from me.

"That, um... won't be possible. I don't get off work until late."

I kept a firm grip on his hand. Not so much that he couldn't get away if he tried, but enough to make it clear that I wasn't giving up so easily.

"It doesn't have to be tonight. Any time will do."

Taking a deep breath, Oliver picked up his toppled chair and perched on the very edge like he was ready to run at a moment's notice.

"Look. What you're suggesting sounds... really nice, but I can't. I work a lot, and when I'm not working I have to be home. Earlier, I mentioned my brother is sick, right? Well, he has Spinal Muscular Atrophy. He needs round the clock care, but an at home nurse is expensive. My mother also works long hours, so whenever I'm not working I have to look after my brother in order to cut down on costs. So, I'm sorry. I'd like to go out with you, but... I can't."

Perhaps it was the shock of rejection that loosened my tongue. Not many people said no to me so I didn't have much practice for how to handle it. Whatever the reason, I found myself speaking before I'd even thought about what to say.

"Bring him along."

Oliver jerked in surprise, knocking over his thankfully empty cup. "What?"

The shock on his face mirrored my own feelings, but once the words were out of my mouth I couldn't take them back. My only option was to push forward with as much feigned confidence as possible. "You have to look after your brother when you're not at work. All right. Bring him along. We can make a day of it."

Oliver stared at me in shock, his petal pink lips hanging open as he tried and failed to form words. "Why... you're... are you sure?"

Was I sure?

Absolutely not.

This whole situation was so far off my usual script, I had no idea what I was doing.

None of that uncertainty showed on my face.

"Of course, I'm going to have to change my plans. A romantic restaurant wouldn't be appropriate, but it can't be that hard to find some family friendly activities in this city."

Oliver didn't immediately reply, staring at me with his eyes so wide the whites were visible all the way around the iris.

"But... I mean, why? You barely know me. Why would you bother going so far?"

Why indeed?

I was asking myself the same question.

Throwing one arm over the back of my chair, I adopted a nonchalant pose. "It's because I want to get to know you. And if this is the only way to do that, then so be it."

So many different emotions played across Oliver's face I couldn't keep track of them.

"If you're sure, then... Rowan doesn't actually get out of the house much. He'd love to spend a day out. So, I guess, okay." The emotion he finally ended on turned out to be a wary sort of excitement. "All right. Yes. If you're sure this is what you want, then it's a date."

We spent a little more time discussing days and times, agreeing on when exactly to meet. I hadn't decided what we were going to do yet, but I asked Oliver about his brother's interests. The boy, Rowan, seemed fairly typical for a fifteen-year-old. He liked action movies, especially ones with monsters and explosions.

I wasn't sure what to do with this information yet, but it at least gave me something to start with.

Eventually, Oliver could no longer ignore his responsibilities and returned to the front counter, leaving me at the table to contemplate what I'd just agreed to.

My plan for the day had been to charm Oliver into my bed. It was meant to be quick, and probably temporary. Instead, it looked like I was going to have to commit a lot more time and effort than I expected.

I automatically watched Oliver as the man set about re-stocking the cups behind the counter, admiring the sure way he moved.

More effort, but worth it.

The coffee machine made a weird noise and Oliver started lecturing it like it was a misbehaving child.

Yes. Definitely worth it.

The bell over the front door dinged as a new guest stepped into the shop. I was so lost in my thoughts that it didn't immediately occur to me what the sound meant. A moment later, as I heard footsteps approaching, the hair on the back of my neck stood on end.

Eva and Gavriil had been specifically instructed to keep everyone away from the shop so I wouldn't be disturbed. There were very few people my bodyguards would have allowed through that door, and none of them would be here for a good reason.

Keeping all emotion off my face, I listened closer to the approaching footsteps. High heels clicked against the linoleum floor, and I immediately knew who I was dealing with.

"Caprice," I said as the woman sat down across from me at the table.

That was it. No greeting passed my lips. There was nothing I could say that would be both polite and truthful.

Sharp red nails tapped against the faux wood tabletop as she stared at me.

"D'Angelo. You were harder to find than I expected. Baltimore isn't your usual territory."

Caprice Vidales, head of the Vidales family, led one of the other most powerful Italian Mafia families on this continent. Still nowhere near as powerful as the Mariano family, she and I had been thorns in each other's sides for years. The woman had her sights set on one day overtaking the Mariano family, but she wouldn't be able to do it alone.

First she tried to get someone from her family married to Alex Mariano, but that had been almost immediately shot down.

Her second plan was for her and I to combine our families so that we could take down the Mariano family together. Her idea was to combine our families through marriage, with her in charge, of course. That hadn't gone as well as she hoped, and she'd never forgiven me.

In the grand scheme of things, I could almost understand her frustration. A few decades ago when homosexuality wasn't as accepted, her plans would have probably worked. Alex and I both would have needed to marry women for the sake of public image, and a woman from her family would have been an ideal choice.

Gay men were really proving to be an insurmountable obstacle for her. One she could have overcome easily if she'd thought to offer a man from her family for marriage. Either Alex or I might have actually accepted that deal, but either there weren't any men in her immediate family that she trusted enough for such a role, or the idea never occurred to her.

I smiled in her general direction, showing too many teeth for the expression to be genuine. "So, what are you doing here? Come to thank me in person for my gift?"

She sniffed in disdain and brushed a lock of poker straight dark hair out of her face. "I don't know what you're talking about."

Dealing with the criminal underworld on a regular basis meant that I was fluent in the language of lies. For example, when someone really didn't know something, they tended to get to the point with simple phrases like "What are you talking about?" A long, formally worded sentence like "I don't know what you're talking about," was usually a sign of lying.

My grin grew wider. "Oh, come now. I made it especially for you. Tell me you at least read the card I attached."

She sneered at me but said nothing.

Still, I could easily imagine her disgusted face when she found Shane's body spread out in pieces on her doorstep. There was no doubt in my mind that she was the one who set my previous lover up to try and kill me. I still wasn't sure if she convinced him after he'd already found his way into my bed, or if he'd been a plant from the start. However, it didn't matter. The outcome was the same.

Shane was dead and Caprice's latest attempt at getting rid of me so she could take over the Bianchi family had failed.

As if sensing my thoughts, she narrowed her sharp eyes at me until they were as thin as dagger blades. "You may not realize, but I've been expanding my business into this area, so I was concerned when I heard you'd been hanging around here. Along with Alex's presence as well, I can't help but wonder what's going on. Has the little prince already got himself into trouble trying to fill daddy's shoes?"

The Vidales family was moving into Baltimore?

It must have been a new move, because this was the first time I was hearing about it.

Either that, or it was a very successful secret.

Baltimore was only a stone's throw from D.C. It was a great location for influencing the country's capital without being right on their doorstep, but that close location also made it a risk. It was much easier to mobilize against an enemy that was practically camped out in your backyard, meaning federal law enforcement could also come after us much easier when we were so close to their headquarters.

Recently, the FBI director had been killed in the line of duty, and there had been a scramble to find a proper replacement. Perhaps this disruption had given Caprice the confidence to try increasing her influence on the country's government.

Could that also be why the Russians were so set on meeting in this area?

Whatever the reason, her involvement in Baltimore could prove problematic for both me and Alex if she interfered with Russian relations. I would need to get rid of her.

Under the table, I fingered the dial of my watch. Oliver was lucky that he hadn't accidentally activated it when he grabbed my wrist earlier. The watch had a hidden compartment that could shoot out poison needles, which were fired by turning and pressing the winding dial in just the right way.

The Bianchi family had always specialized in drugs. My great grandmother invented the poison on these needles, and the formula for the antidote lay locked away in our family vault. The table was only a few feet wide. At such close proximity, I wouldn't even need to aim. One prick from a poisoned needle and she would be dead within minutes.

Problem solved.

However, killing her would incite backlash from the Vidales family. I was already trying to prevent a war with the Russians. I couldn't afford to initiate a war between Italian families at the same time.

I let go of my watch and placed both hands on the table in front of me.

"My business is my own, and doesn't concern you. Stop sending assassins after me and I'll stop returning them to you in pieces. Understand?"

After so many years of association, I was immune to her intimidation tactics. The conversation was over and we both knew it. She stood to leave, but not without one last parting comment.

"Don't bother buying anything here,"

she said as she left. "The drinks aren't worth the price."

Then she was finally gone, and the bell over the door marked her departure with a merry jingle.

I breathed a sigh of relief, but deep down I knew I couldn't relax. Usually, Caprice was a problem I just ignored, but this time I might need to find a more permanent solution for her.

At least we'd been too far away for Oliver to hear us. I didn't need to scare away my latest conquest before I'd even won him.

Nodding at Oliver on my way out, I found Eva and Gavriil waiting for me just a few steps away on the sidewalk.

"Sorry, sir," Eva said as they walked with me to the car. "You told us to keep everyone away from the shop, but we couldn't..."

I held up a hand to cut her off. "No, you did the right thing. Caprice Vidales can't be chased away like some ordinary citizen. If she was determined to come inside, nothing short of death would have stopped her, and we don't need that right now."

Gavriil opened the car door for me, and

handed me an unmarked manila folder once I was settled inside.

"That's everything we've found about Oliver Grant so far," Eva explained as she took her place in the shotgun seat. "He seems to be just an ordinary civilian, but we can keep digging if you'd like."

As I opened the folder, Gavriil slipped in behind the wheel and started the car.

"Keep looking," I said as I glanced over the picture of Oliver on the first page. "Shawn also seemed like an ordinary civilian, right up until he tried to kill me. Oh, and while you're at it, get me everything there is to know about Spinal Muscular Atrophy."

If Eva or Gavriil found this request strange, they knew better than to question it, and I was left to read in peace.

The picture of Oliver wasn't very good. The harsh lighting threw his scars into stark relief and dulled the colors of his eyes. Scowling at it, I quickly turned the page. Most of the folder contained information I already knew, but one page stuffed right in the middle of everything caught my eye.

"Oh, now this is interesting."

CHAPTER EIGHT

Oliver

"NO, ASHES, YOU don't understand," I practically shouted as I tugged at my hair. "What the hell was I thinking, agreeing to this."

Ashes sat hunched over their workbench, meticulously bending a wire with a pair of pliers into a complex Celtic knot. In middle school, Ashes had adopted the Goth aesthetic and never let it go. Even now, at the age of twenty-two, they still dressed in all black with spikes and chains for decoration and several tattoos along their arms. Their hair was dyed a black so dark it looked blue and hung in a messy disarray that ended just past their chin.

I remembered the first time I helped Ashes dye their hair. We'd made a mess with the cheap box dye and gotten in so much trouble. After years of practice, they'd gotten much better at coloring their hair. So much so, that even I often forgot their hair wasn't naturally that color.

At first glance, many people mistook my friend for some sort of satanic cultist who tortured animals in their backyard. Most would never know that Ashes was actually one of the nicest souls I'd ever met, and the only thing they ever tortured was their soldering iron when they obsessed over a new jewelry project.

Even now, they were barely listening to me, too focused on their latest creation. However, I'd already repeated myself so many times that they knew just how to respond, even if they weren't paying attention.

"You agreed to the date 'cause the guy was hot, and Rowan would love the opportunity to get out of the house and do something fun."

"Yeah, I know." With a huff, I threw myself down on the ratty couch in the far corner of the workshop. "And that's all still true, but what am I doing? I haven't been on a date in..."

"High school senior year," Ashes reminded me without looking up from their work. "Jaxson Miller."

"Oh, God. Right." I pressed a pillow over my face, hoping it would smother me. "That was a nightmare."

Ashes snorted and their pliers slipped off the wire they were working with. Putting everything down, they finally looked up at me. A jeweler's loupe sat on the bridge of their nose, a tool they often used when working with particularly intricate pieces, and it made one of their eyes look comically bigger than the other.

"Nightmare? That's an understatement. The guy went out with you on a dare, like the cliché villain in a teen movie. His friends were secretly following behind and recording you."

The pillow hit the floor with a swirl of dust when I threw it at Ashes. "Yes, I know. Thank you for reminding me why I should never trust people. Especially not with my brother. Remember that other guy I dated for, like, a week. What was his name?"

"Robert something-or-other."

"Right. Forgot. I tried to block every memory of him from my mind after he only pretended to be nice to my brother as a way to get me to sleep with him. Ugh. Ableist bastard."

The couch bounced when Ashes sat next to me, carefully storing the jeweler's loupe in their pocket so I could clearly see both their eyes. "But that was all High School shit. It happened years ago. This guy isn't some stupid teen. He's probably a lot more mature than any of them were. How old is he anyway?"

"I don't even know that much about him. Literally, all I know is his first name." I fished my phone out of my pocket and shoved it at my friend. "Here. I managed to snap a pic when he wasn't looking. What'd you think?"

Ashes took the phone, studying it this way and that, before a grin spread over their face. "This guy's got some real big dick energy going on."

I slapped their shoulder, accidentally nicking my knuckles on one of the studs on their collar. "Ashes. Stop being a thirsty bitch and help me."

"Fine, fine," they agreed, though they

continued to chuckle to themselves. "Well, judging by the way his hair gets a little lighter on the sides, I think there might be some gray hidden in that lush darkness. He's probably a little older than he seems. I'm guessing late thirties."

An age gap hadn't even crossed my mind. It hadn't mattered when there were so many other gaps between us, but now it seemed like a pressing matter.

I clutched my phone to my chest when Ashes handed it back, mindful of the cracked screen. "Is that too much? I'm only twenty-two. No wonder he seemed so much more self-assured than the other guys I've gone out with. He's probably got plenty of experience. I've never even dated someone more than a few weeks. What could I offer that would interest him?"

Ashes grabbed my chin and forced me to look at them. "Hey. You're spiraling. Focus."

For a moment, I swore I could feel the heat of fire on my skin, but I knew it was only an illusion brought on by my heightened emotions. I sucked in a few deep breaths, slowly counting them out in my head, and felt my pulse calm down.

A cool breeze from Ashes' air

conditioning drifted over my skin.

"Thanks."

"No problem. But, seriously, you shouldn't worry so much. I doubt this guy cares about the age gap. You look your age, so I'm sure he already realizes that you're younger. And something about you must interest him, or else he wouldn't have asked you out."

"Yeah," I said, though I still wasn't reassured. Ashes seemed to sense that I had more to say and waited for me to continue. "There was one more thing."

"There always is. What is it?"

"Well..." I tipped my head back and forth, wondering how to explain what I'd seen. "There was this woman who he talked to at the coffee shop."

Ashes scowled, and for a moment the scary Satanist that they were so often accused of being almost seemed plausible. "You mean he was chatting someone else up right after asking you out?"

"Not like that." I thought back to the woman who'd stormed into the shop and just sat at D'Angelo's table without so much as a hello. "It wasn't a... how do I put this... a *friendly* conversation. They obviously knew each other, but the tension between them wasn't the good kind. I don't know. Something about it just rubbed me the wrong way."

I tried to explain the interaction I'd witnessed with as much detail as possible, but since I hadn't heard what they were talking about, there wasn't much I could say with certainty.

Ashes thought about it for a moment. "Maybe he's married. I'd be pissed, too, if I found my husband running around picking up younger men."

"Oh, God," I groaned and hung my head in my hands. "Don't put that possibility in my mind. There are enough obstacles between D'Angelo and I already."

While Ashes' suggestion was possible, I doubted it was true. D'Angelo and the woman weren't strangers, but they weren't particularly familiar, either.

No, it must be something else, but I had no idea what.

An alarm on my phone beeped. I needed to leave soon so I could take over Rowan's care from the nurse. My shift at the coffee shop had ended early enough that I could spend a few hours hanging out with my friend. There was no telling when I'd be able to spend time with Ashes again, and now I'd wasted all our time together rambling.

I opened my mouth, ready to apologize for wasting Ashes time, but they predicted what I was about to do and cut me off.

"Don't. I won't accept an apology. Not for this. Talking about problems is exactly what friends are for. Now, you want my advice? Go on the date. See what this guy is about. If he turns out to be a scumbag, then we'll binge on ice cream and bitch about him afterward. But, who knows. Maybe you'll get lucky."

Eyes hidden behind pink colored contacts regarded me up and down for a moment.

"Honestly, getting dicked down would probably do you some good."

Ashes cackled as I slapped their shoulder several times.

"You are horrible. I don't know why I'm friends with you."

Despite my words, we both knew I didn't mean it. There was no better friend I could possibly have, and I was grateful everyday. If my date with D'Angelo didn't work out, I wouldn't be alone.

But, Ashes was right. Maybe it would work out. I wouldn't know until I tried.

What was the worst that could happen?

CHAPTER NINE

Oliver

THE DAY OF our date came sooner than expected. Before I knew it, I was stepping off the bus near Baltimore's inner harbor.

"Are you sure I was invited, too?" Rowan asked after we'd maneuvered his wheelchair off the bus. There was a wheelchair lift, but it rattled so badly I was just waiting for the day it finally broke down. Luckily, today was not that day, and we managed to get him on and off the bus without too many problems.

Other than the stares and side-eyes we received whenever we went out together, but those were expected at this point. Two brothers, one scarred and one handicapped, always drew attention when we were seen together.

"Yeah, bud," I said, while looking at the directions on my phone. "You were definitely invited. We specifically discussed it."

Figuring out which way we needed to go to meet with D'Angelo, I started walking down the sidewalk, but Rowan didn't follow me. His chair stayed rooted in place, directly under the bus stop sign.

"I'm sorry to interfere with your date. That's what this was supposed to be, right? This guy asked you out, but you had to bring me along since there's no one else to watch me."

I kneeled down on the sidewalk in front of him, placing my hands on the arms of his chair. "Hey. No, you're not interfering. In fact, you're doing me a favor." He gave me a skeptical look, but I could see the spark of hope in his eyes, the same hazel color as my own. "I would never want to date someone who didn't get along with my brother. With you here, I'll be able to tell if this guy is worth dating before I get too invested. If anything, you're saving me a lot of time and heartbreak. So, you've got to help me out and tell me what you think of him. Okay?"

He nodded with more enthusiasm this time. "All right. And, if he gives you any trouble, I'll run over his foot."

"See. I knew you'd have my back. Now, let's get going. We're already running a bit late."

D'Angelo was already waiting for us exactly where he'd said he'd be. He cut an attractive figure, standing beside the inner harbor and looking out over the water. Once again dressed in an all black suit, he had chosen an outfit made of a light cotton material to compensate for the warm summer weather. He seemed to be going for a more relaxed look with the first few buttons undone to expose his collarbone and a sliver of his chest.

I let my eyes wander, admiring the dark complexion of his olive toned skin, and wondered if he'd ever consider wearing something other than black. White would look really good with his coloring.

It also made me self-conscious of my own outfit. I was a fan of color, and when I wasn't forced to wear a uniform for work, I incorporated as many colors into my clothes as possible. Not knowing where we were going, I'd chosen a mix of casual and formal. Most of my clothes were second hand, so I didn't have a lot to choose from. The black and gold waistcoat had been a lucky thrift shop find, while the red plaid pants were a gift from Ashes.

Supposedly, according to my friend, the tight cut of the pants made my legs look good. I'd decided to take their word for it, because I couldn't see any difference. My legs were my legs, no matter what cloth they were wrapped in.

D'Angelo turned to face us as we approached, and for the first time I noticed the woman standing next to him. She kept a bit of space between them, so I hadn't realized they were together at first, but there was no mistaking the focus of her attention.

A thousand thoughts raced through my mind.

Was I missing something?

Had I misinterpreted the situation?

I feared things were about to get awkward and tried to speak normally when I greeted him. "Hey, sorry we're late.

The bus was running behind.”

“It’s no problem. We’re not on any schedule.”

He grabbed my hand and brought it to his lips, brushing a light kiss over the back of my fingers.

I blushed and tried to control the urge to shiver. Such a small thing shouldn’t affect me so strongly, but it was the first time we’d ever actually touched skin to skin.

In fact, the more I thought about it, I realized it was the first time in years I’d made skin contact with someone other than my family or Ashes.

To my surprise, D’Angelo then turned to my brother and introduced himself.

“Hello. You must be Rowan. Oliver has told me a lot about you.”

The defiant look on Rowan’s eye filled me with pride. My little brother wouldn’t be cowed, not even when a man who stood well over six feet loomed over him.

“And you’re D’Angelo,” Rowan said with his chin held high. “Oliver’s told me about you, too.”

For a moment, I feared D’Angelo would be offended by Rowan’s tone, but my date only smiled. “I’m glad to hear your brother's been thinking about me." Glancing over at me, he winked, like he knew exactly which gutter my thoughts strayed into whenever his name was mentioned.

Then, however, he turned back to Rowan with a serious expression. "I hope you don't mind, but I brought someone along to accompany us today." He gestured toward the woman standing just a step behind him. "This is nurse Malory. She's a private caregiver and has experience with SMA. I've brought her along today in case you need anything."

Rowan and I were both shocked. We knew the price of a private nurse, since our family employed one regularly.

"Oh, um, thanks," Rowan stuttered, before wheeling himself over to speak with the nurse.

As the two introduced themselves, I stepped up to D'Angelo's side.

"You didn't have to do that. I can take care of him."

D'Angelo's arm slipped around my waist and pulled me closer. "Ah, but I'm greedy." His hand settled on my hip and his pale blue eyes shone like sunlight reflecting off ice. "I want all your attention on me."

I gaped at him, not knowing what to say. Out of habit, I reached up to tug my bangs over the left side of my face, but he stopped me before I could.

"Don't hide your eyes. I want to see them."

My face burned hot with embarrassment, and I stared down at the sidewalk. "It's not my eyes I'm trying to hide."

He didn't say anything in response, and my heart sank.

What could he say?

My scars were impossible to ignore.

A strange sensation on my left cheek made me jump. I stared up at D'Angelo in shock, holding my cheek with one hand. My skin was slightly damp.

He'd just kissed my cheek. His lips had brushed against my scarred skin without flinching. No one had ever done that before. Not even my mother. As a kid, whenever she kissed me, it was always on the right cheek.

I never realized the scars were so sensitive. The place where D'Angelo had kissed still tingled, and I could practically feel the exact shape of his mouth.

Still, he didn't say a word. Just smirked at me before stepping away to speak with Rowan.

I remained rooted in place, too shocked to move or speak. Already this date wasn't going how I expected, and my heart felt like it was going to vibrate right out of my chest.

Rowan's excited voice broke through my stupor and brought me back to reality.

"The ships? All of them? Really? I've always wanted to go."

He was practically bouncing in his wheelchair. Whatever D'Angelo said had made him happier than I'd seen in a long time.

"I'm glad you approved of my choice," D'Angelo said in all seriousness. "The nearest one is just up ahead. The USS Constellation. We can start there, unless there's a different one you'd rather see first."

"No, that's fine. Let's go."

Rowan led the way, eagerly pushing his wheelchair down the street. The nurse stayed nearby, always on hand, but far enough away to not be intrusive. D'Angelo walked beside Rowan's chair, continuing their discussion about ships.

With a sinking feeling, I slipped in beside D'Angelo and whispered so only the other man could hear me. "Where are we going?"

Eagerly pulling me closer, D'Angelo settled his arm over my shoulder. "There's a bunch of historic naval ships displayed here in the harbor, with tours to go explore them. I figured it seemed like something a teenage boy who likes monster movies and explosions might be interested in."

It was exactly as I feared. Biting my lip, I swallowed past the knot of disappointment and dread in my throat.

"I should have warned you. We've tried bringing Rowan here before, but the ships aren't very wheelchair friendly. Most of them are only accessible by gangplanks, which are too steep and narrow for him to navigate. Even the ships he can access, he'll be stuck on the top deck since the bottom parts of the ship require a ladder to reach. He won't be able to do most of the stuff."

I expected disappointment, or maybe even anger, so I was surprised when D'Angelo just calmly squeezed my shoulder.

"It's fine. They've done some remodeling to make the ships more handicap accessible. He should have no problem."

"What?"

I glanced out over the harbor at the looming figure of the nearest ship floating in the water. Just as D'Angelo had said, the gangplank onto the ship looked different than I remembered. Wider, and with a much shallower incline that would be easy for a wheelchair to manage.

"But, I never heard about any renovations, and I usually try to keep an eye on these things."

"Well, the changes were recent," D'Angelo waved away my confusion. "Perhaps you just hadn't heard about it yet. It's lucky for us, though. Come on. I've booked tours for all of the ships, plus the lighthouse."

Despite D'Angelo's claim that he wanted my attention, he spent an unexpected amount of time talking with Rowan. It was just general conversation, like favorite movies and books, and other places in Baltimore that were worth checking out. Yet, it was more than I had expected.

In the past, even people who seemed to be accepting of my brother usually just ignored him as much as possible. I expected this date to be the same, and would have considered it a success so long as D'Angelo wasn't outright cruel to Rowan.

For D'Angelo to actually take the effort to engage my brother and make him feel like a part of the outing, rather than just a necessary tag-along, was far better than I'd even dared to hope for.

The first ship we visited was the oldest of the bunch, and reminded me of a pirate ship. A tour guide walked us through the ship, explaining its history and giving brief lessons about how sailing worked nearly two hundred years ago.

The contraption that was used to lower Rowan's chair down into the bottom half of the ship reminded me of elevators in mineshafts. It was hoisted by hand on a pulley system and couldn't hold more than two people at a time.

I didn't realize how worried I'd been until Rowan safely reached the lower half of the ship. It had worked, just as D'Angelo promised. We finished the tour of the first ship and moved on to the next one without issue, and I began to realize that D'Angelo might be much more dependable than I first thought.

When he promised something, it happened.

The first ship was my favorite, but the others were interesting as well. By the second ship, it was clear that Rowan was too invested in what the tour guide was saying to pay much attention to us, so D'Angelo and I had a chance to talk. I told him about how I first met Ashes in elementary school, as they were the only kid who didn't bully me over my scars. That, of course, led to a discussion about what caused my scars in the first place.

"It was a house fire," I said, instinctively bracing against the memory of pain.

My arm was looped through D'Angelo's with my hand resting in the crook of his elbow. As soon as the word "fire" left my lips, my skin began to feel hot all over, and I gripped the sleeve of his suit hard enough to crease the fabric.

"I was only seven. I was supposed to be at a neighbor's birthday party, but I came home early because the other kids were making fun of me. Rowan was only a few months old. As soon as he was diagnosed, my dad left. I guess he didn't want to deal with a handicapped child. Seven year olds can be cruel. My father was gone, and my new brother was disabled. It gave them too much ammunition. They couldn't help teasing me. I didn't want them to see me cry, so I just left and went home since it was only a few houses away."

So wrapped up in my memory, I didn't notice the coil of rope lying stacked on the floor. I nearly tripped, but D'Angelo guided me around the obstacle. He didn't say a word, just silently kept his arm looped with mine and let me talk.

"I was tired from crying and fell asleep in my room. When I woke up, everything was on fire. I think the fire department later said something about faulty wiring in the walls, but I'm not sure. We had fire drills at school occasionally. I knew I needed to leave so I started trying to make my way downstairs on my own. One thing they never get right in movies. How loud fire really is. The air is so dry it seems to amplify every vibrational echo until the crackle of burning wood is all you can hear."

At this point in the story, my chest felt heavy and my breathing strained. I had to pause and step to the side of the ship to look out over the water and catch my breath.

D'Angelo joined me, peering over the railing as well so our reflections floated next to each other in the harbor.

"Where was the rest of your family? Surely your neighbor would have told them that you went home."

"I don't know," I shook my head, dislodging the image of fire dancing in front of my eyes and focusing on the salty smell of the harbor. "It wouldn't have mattered, though. My mother and grandmother were outside the house when the fire started. It spread so fast, the whole house was burning by the time they realized what was happening. I'm told that my mother tried to go back inside, but the fire department stopped her."

My lungs felt clear again, no longer choked with the memory of smoke, so I stood taller and looked D'Angelo in the eye.

"I'm not sure how I heard my brother

crying over the sound of the fire, but I did. I remember turning away from the stairs to go to his room instead and picking him up out of his crib, but after that it's all kind of a blur. The smoke was getting to me by then and I was having trouble staying on my feet. I'm told I came stumbling out the front door with my clothes on fire and my brother clutched in my arms."

I gestured at the scar on my face. "Treatment for my injuries took months, but I'm glad if someone had to get burned it was me. Rowan didn't need to deal with this on top of his own illness. I should warn you now, the scars on my face aren't the only ones. Just the most prominent. If that bothers you, then you should walk away now. I've had someone throw up when they saw me shirtless before, and I'd rather not have to deal with that kind of blow to my ego again."

D'Angelo regarded me for a moment with a serious eye, then suddenly started unbuttoning his shirt.

"Wh-what are you doing?" I stuttered and tried to pull his shirt closed.

He shrugged me off, but he didn't remove his shirt all the way, just pulled it aside enough to reveal the left side of his chest. A cluster of small round scars marred the skin there.

"My grandfather used to put his cigarettes out on me because he thought it would toughen me up."

Without even blinking over such an admission, he rolled up one of his sleeves to expose his forearm and the long scar running all the way from wrist to elbow.

"The first person I slept with stabbed me with a kitchen knife because I wouldn't agree to marry them. Scars are just skin with memories. There's nothing inherently wrong or ugly about them, and there's no reason to be ashamed of them. If anything, people without scars should be the ones ashamed. It means they haven't really done anything worth remembering."

I ran one finger over the scar on his arm, feeling the way the flesh rose up like a rope embedded under his skin. A strange desire overcame me. I wanted to kiss it.

I wanted to kiss him.

On instinct, I leaned closer to him until I could feel the natural heat radiating off his body. He was taller than me, so kissing him would be difficult, but if I tugged on his lapel I could probably convince him to lean down.

I would have kissed him right then on the deck of the USCG Cutter, if it weren't for Rowan's timely return. The sound of my brother's voice reminded me that we were in public where anyone could see us. Now was not the time for intimacy.

Running my hand over his suit, I tried to smooth out the wrinkles I'd left in the fabric, but it was a lost cause. We returned to the tour guide, a little more rumpled than we had been before.

Out of all the ships in the harbor, the last one, the USS Torsk, was the most modern. At least, modern in comparison to the other ships, being only eighty years old.

It was also a submarine, which automatically made it Rowan's favorite. He was starting to get tired. I could tell from his slumped posture in the chair, but he refused to take a break. The nurse hovered close by Rowan's side, assisting him however she could, and I found myself immensely grateful that D'Angelo had brought her. I was used to taking care of my brother, but it was also nice to let someone else take the responsibility.

Inside, the submarine was much darker than the other ships had been. Every doorway had a six-inch bulkhead that would have been a nightmare to maneuver a wheelchair over, if not for the boards laid over each one to create a small ramp.

The control room of the submarine was definitely the most interesting part of the whole thing, but it was narrow and small. There was just enough room for Rowan, the nurse, and the tour guide, so D'Angelo and I waited in the hallway outside.

"Thanks for this," I whispered to him, conscious of how my voice echoed off the metal. "You didn't have to go this far, but Rowan is having a blast. It's been so long since he got out of the house. He's going to be talking about this day for months."

D'Angelo leaned over so his mouth hovered near my ear, keeping his voice to a whisper as well. "Maybe it's selfish to say, but I didn't do it for him."

Before I could respond, he tugged me by my wrist into another side room. Just as cramped as everywhere else on a submarine, it seemed to have once been the weapons room. My back pressed against the wall between two empty missile silos.

D'Angelo wasn't even trying to crowd me, but the size of the room didn't give him much choice. Surrounded by metal walls on all sides, his much larger frame towered over me and blocked out the submarine's minimal lighting.

He ran a hand through his hair, dark strands slipping through tan fingers. Up close, I could see the hints of gray at his temple that Ashes had pointed out. The thick dark hair did a good job hiding the color, but it was still there as a reminder of the gap between us.

"After just a few minutes of knowing you, I could tell you were a family-oriented person," he explained, still whispering. "You'd never give me the time of day if I didn't get along with your brother."

He pressed a little closer, so he was practically caging me against the wall. I placed a hand on his chest, and he fell still, waiting to see what I would do.

If I pushed him away, I felt certain that he would leave.

That knowledge gave me the

confidence to pop open one of the buttons on his shirt, exposing more of his chest.

His blue eyes seemed to spark in the dark.

"You know, it's a very fine line." He leaned in until our foreheads touched. "I want to show interest in the things that matter to you, but a man of my age showing too much interest in a fifteen-year-old boy is potentially problematic in a lot of ways. Sometimes, I feel like there's no winning. You really have set up a challenge for me."

Keeping one hand on his chest, I let my other one run though his hair. "And what age is that? Now that we're this close, I've noticed you've got some gray here. My friend was right, you are older than you look."

I gasped in surprise when he grabbed my wrist and pinned it against the wall near my head. The hand I still had on his chest stiffened, instinctively ready to push him away.

He fell still again, waiting for my reaction.

It wasn't the first time someone had grabbed me, but it was the first time I felt safe while also trapped. Maybe it was the fact that I still knew I could leave whenever I wanted that made staying so exciting.

Just to make things clear, I fisted my hand in his shirt and pulled him a little closer.

His grin was so sinful he could have rivaled the devil.

"Teasing a man about his age," he said as he wrapped his fingers around my other wrist. "That could get you into a lot of trouble. I'm only thirty-eight. Hardly what I'd call old."

With slow, deliberate movements, he brought my other wrist up to the wall as well so both of my arms were pinned by my head.

I shivered even though I wasn't cold. Something hot twisted deep in my stomach and for a moment, I lost all feeling in my legs.

"Twenty-two," I supplied my own age. "That's not a problem, is it?"

"Only if it's a problem for you."

I quickly shook my head, feeling the metal wall scrape against the back of my scalp.

"Good..." He was so close now I could feel his breath on my lips. "Because I really don't want to stop."

I waited with bated breath for him to kiss me, but it never came. We were so close we were practically breathing the same air, yet he refused to close the remaining distance between us.

Desperation sat like a pit in my stomach. I licked my lips and tried not to squirm.

"Well? If you don't want to stop, then why aren't you doing anything?"

His laughter was little more than a single puff of air. "I could ask you the same thing."

Finally realizing what he was waiting for, I surged forward as far as my trapped wrists would allow and claimed a desperate, hungry kiss.

The moment our lips touched, fire seemed to burn through my veins, but for the first time, I didn't mind the heat.

CHAPTER TEN

D'Angelo

THE KISS DIDN'T last as long as I would have liked. We were still in public after all, and Oliver's brother would soon come looking for us. So, after a few minutes, we were forced to pull away and quickly tug our clothes back into place. We still probably looked a bit flushed, and anyone with half a brain could probably tell what we'd been doing, but we returned to Oliver's brother just in time for the tour to end.

After visiting the last boat, as well as the lighthouse that stood at the end of the harbor, I offered to take both brothers to lunch. Rowan was allowed to choose, and appropriate for a fifteen-year-old boy, he chose a nearby restaurant called *Dick's Last Resort*. I was ready to agree, but Oliver quickly steered us away and insisted on going to an Italian place instead.

"Rowan doesn't know this, but that place is notorious," Oliver whispered to me during the short walk to the restaurant. "It's kinda got the vibe of a standup comedy club. Guests are often insulted, and for Rowan and I... that kind of atmosphere is just asking for trouble."

I agreed, and without further discussion we went to the Italian restaurant instead. It was very Americanized, and not comparable to real Italian food, but good enough to ensure that the rest of the date ended well.

When we finally parted and I met back up with Eva and Gavriil, who had been loitering around nearby the whole time, I was satisfied with how my relationship was progressing with Oliver.

CHAPTER ELEVEN

D'Angelo

MY GOOD MOOD following my date with Oliver and his brother lasted all the way until my meeting with the Russian representatives the following day.

Although it was the Russians who had insisted on meeting in Baltimore, they remained tightlipped about why they chose the location, or what the actual issue was. That left me eventually standing outside of the American Visionary Art Museum and not entirely sure what I would face at the meeting. The museum was on the southern side of the Inner Harbor. I could see the masts of the ships I'd visited with Oliver and Rowan from my position on the front steps.

Less than twenty-four hours, and I stood in practically in the same place, yet my mindset couldn't have been more different. There was nothing soft or intimate about the role of the Bianchi family leader.

"It's quaint, isn't it?" someone said when they stepped up beside me.

I vaguely recognized the voice, though it took a moment for me to place the face.

She was known only by her surname, Aslanov. No one knew her first name, and I'd never needed to know, so I never went to the trouble of looking. So blonde her hair nearly looked white, the thick curls were pulled back into a painfully strict ponytail. She was tall for a woman, and in heels she nearly equaled me in height.

We'd met twice before. Once when I was very young, my mother brought me to Russia to meet my relatives on her side. Then once at my indoctrination as the head of the Bianchi family. Both times, she had been standing as the Pahkan's right-hand-woman.

She was an accomplished middleman

in the Russian Mafia.

To see her alone now was... odd, and slightly terrifying. If the leader of the Russian mafia was personally involved, then there was no hope of this incident blowing over easily.

"What's quaint?" I asked while looking around for Aslanov's security. Just like my own bodyguards, a pair of armed men loitered around the area. To the casual observer, they probably just looked like museum guests, but I recognized the stance of someone armed and ready for action. It was the same stance my own bodyguards wore like a uniform every day.

They were also entirely superfluous, and probably just for show. Aslanov didn't actually need bodyguards. There was a rumor that she'd once killed an entire squad of secret service agents, as well as the dignitary they were protecting, with only the heel of her shoe. It was a ludicrously violent story, and I absolutely believed it.

Aslanov pointed out to the other side of the harbor. "Little Italy. The alliteration just rolls off the tongue."

She didn't grin, but there was a gleam

in her eyes that reminded me of a shark's smile.

Little Italy?

I hadn't really thought about it, but just on the other side of the harbor lay a neighborhood that had been established by the Italian immigrants who first came to the area. It was also once a stronghold for the Italian mafia, though we had moved out of the area by the mid twentieth century. Now, it was mostly just a regular neighborhood with an interesting backstory.

Was this meant to be some sort of hint?

A threat?

I'd wondered about the location of the meeting since learning the address. An art museum seemed like an odd choice.

The American Visionary Art Museum wasn't a particularly big building, certainly nothing compared to the skyscrapers of New York, but it had an odd design. Mostly cylindrical, the outside was almost entirely covered by a swirling silver mosaic.

I couldn't see a reason to meet at such a place, but perhaps the building wasn't important. Perhaps the real message was in the location, lurking just across the water from Italian territory.

Aslanov turned away from the harbor and headed inside the museum. "Come. We'll talk inside."

Beyond the front doors, the building's silver mosaic continued along the floor. A large staircase curved up the wall of the circular main room, with irregularly shaped doorways leading into smaller galleries. The museum showcased only Outsider Art, and displayed an eclectic collection of techniques and styles. There seemed to be no unifying theme other than "unexpected". Nothing was ever quite what it seemed like it should be.

I followed Aslanov up the staircase, trying to keep her and her bodyguards in sight at all times. The museum was still open, so other guests wandered around, but in the middle of a weekday it wasn't particularly busy.

A statue hung suspended in the air above the heart of the main staircase. From below, it looked like an odd chandelier. Just a twisted mess of metal and glass that made no sense. Yet, as we climbed the stairs and I was able to view the statue from every angle, I realized it was actually a man.

The main body of the statue was bronze, with large wings of silver metal and colored glass sprouting from his back. The man's body was contorted in pain while his wings twisted around him.

It was a fallen angel, or maybe the image of Icarus, frozen in time as it plummeted toward earth.

At the top of the building, and through several galleries, Aslanov brought me to an exhibit that was marked "closed". It seemed to be a new exhibit, still in the process of being installed. The exhibit consisted of an entire room. Illuminated mostly by blacklight, glowing neon sculptures and glow-in-the-dark paint contrasted with the black background. Consisting primarily of purple, pink, and blue, the room looked like an alien forest straight off a sci-fi movie set.

A stray thought entered my mind that this would be a great place to bring Oliver for a second date. I didn't know much about Outsider Art, other than the fact that it was made by "self-taught" artists and didn't conform to conventional art standards. None of this meant anything to me, but Oliver would probably appreciate it a lot more than I could. Listening to him explain what made the artwork significant would make the whole experience more interesting.

The daydream lasted only a moment, and I focused back on my task at hand.

A faux-stone structure covered most of the back wall. It looked like a distorted human face, with a gaping mouth forming a cave. Teeth the size of my head lined the outer rim of the cave, and a stone tongue created a sitting table inside the open mouth. Glowing teal water dripped from the face's eyes and ran down its cheeks into pools along the floor.

While I was sure there was a deeper meaning behind the artistic design, I couldn't see it. The whole thing just creeped me out.

Sitting at the stone-tongue-table with Aslanov, I ignored the rest of the room. The purple-hued blacklight made her white suit glow, and threw her eyes into shadows so they looked like a pair of dark voids sitting in the middle of her face.

"You're probably wondering why I've insisted on meeting here," she said, flashing me with a cold-as-ice smile as soon as I sat down.

I adjusted the cuffs of my jacket, subtly making sure my watch with the hidden poison needles was exposed. "The museum is an odd choice, but much better than meeting in a cold, dirty warehouse in the middle of the night. I swear, some people have no creativity when it comes to these sorts of things."

She obviously wasn't talking about the museum, but I wouldn't be baited into playing her game. If she wanted to talk about why we were meeting in Baltimore, then she would have to approach the topic herself. I wasn't going to ask.

Shadowed eyes glared at me for a moment, and I didn't meet her gaze and busied myself dusting off my suit. Unlike her white suit, my all black outfit disappeared in the blacklight. I was aware of every speck of lint on my clothes, and fought the urge to pluck at the fibers.

Eventually, Aslanov had no choice but to continue the conversation on her own.

"This isn't the first time our people have met in this city. Fifteen years ago, we tried to set up a trade deal with your *Mafia King.*' It failed because someone in your organization betrayed all of us and stole the shipment we sent over. They were never found, and a war nearly broke out between us."

It wasn't an accusation, but it was close. My bodyguards stationed around the room were on high alert, while I kept a close watch on Aslanov's hands. If she was going to kill me, her hands were the first things that would have to move.

"Since that is suspiciously close to what happened this time, let me guess... you assume history is repeating itself?"

Her fist clenched on the table and I tensed, ready to react if she attacked me. "After fifteen years, our Pahkan has graciously decided to give you another chance. Relations between our organizations have always been tense, yet you seem determined to make us your enemy despite our efforts."

I was no stranger to the rocky relationship between the Russian and Italian mafia. It was the reason I existed, after all. A few decades ago, the two sides had been at each other's throats, until a truce was called and sealed with my parent's marriage. Since then, peace still remained, but it held on only by the most fragile threads.

"Don't try to lecture me about my own

history. I'm well aware of how fragile the peace between us is. However, I also know that things have changed. The *Mafia King*, David Russo, is dead, and Alex Mariano has taken over. I was the leader of the Bianchi family fifteen years ago, but I was still young and relatively new to my position so I wasn't involved with the deal. With so many differences, there's no way the same person is responsible for your missing shipment now."

Faster than a striking snake, Alanov's hand shot out and grabbed my wrist. Her fingers lay right over my watch so I couldn't activate the trigger for the hidden needles, and her grip was strong enough to bruise bone.

The metallic sound of weapons being drawn and cocked echoed around the room. My bodyguards and Aslanov's bodyguards were all pointing guns at each other, ready to turn the art installation into a bloodbath at a moment's notice.

"It may not be the same person, but it's the same problem," Aslanov hissed as she slammed my wrist against the table. Barely audible over the cold rage in her voice, was the sound of gears snapping. The mechanism hidden in my watch had broken.

"Your *Mafia King* has left your house a mess, and his son is incapable of cleaning it up. It's obvious your organization is too incompetent to handle this. I'm here to take care of this problem once and for all. We will be given full access to Baltimore's harbor, and you will pay reprimands for what you have stolen, and stay out of our way. Understood."

She let me go and calmly leaned back in her seat.

Although my heart beat rapidly in my chest, I remained calm and frowned down at my watch as if pouting over a broken toy.

"So many big plans you have. And what about me? Any plans for the Bianchi family?"

I removed my watch and examined it. Yep, definitely broken. I could probably remove the needles, but there was no safe way to deploy them.

She dismissed me almost immediately. "Your family isn't worth mentioning, but the Pahkan likes you purely because of blood ties. So, you'll become a marriage trophy, following in your mother's footsteps as a sacrifice for peace."

Her words were not a proposition. They were a command. She fully expected everything to happen exactly as she said. There was probably already a hit squad with their sights on Alex, and a plane fueled up at the nearest airport waiting to ship me off to Russia.

Whatever I decided to do in the next thirty seconds would determine everyone's future.

With my right hand, I blatantly reached for the knife hidden up my sleeve. Aslanov caught my wrist before I'd moved more than an inch.

"Don't be a fool. I'll kill you before you even unsheathe that blade."

I grinned at her. "Not my style. I didn't get where I am by being a fool. I know I can't beat you in a head-to-head fight."

While she'd been focused on my right hand, I'd used my left to slip one of the needles from the broken remains of my watch. I grabbed her hand that was still holding my wrist, and watched her pupils dilate when she felt the prick of the needle against her skin.

"What?" She pulled her hand back and looked down at the small drop of blood staining her white suit. "How did you..."

I held up the needle between two fingers. "You were careless. Breaking my watch only destroyed the deployment mechanism. The poison was still intact."

"But you..." She gaped at me, eyes zeroing in on the drop of blood rolling down my palm. "You've poisoned yourself as well."

The needles were small, sharp and double sided. Without the watch to deploy them, there was no way to handle them without pricking my own skin as well.

"Yes." I sighed and shook my head over the drop of blood sitting on my palm. "Annoying, but harmless. Did you really think I would carry around something that could just as easily kill me as my enemies? That poison is an invention by my family. Of course, I'm immune."

She seethed, but I held up my uninjured hand before she could speak.

"Don't get too upset. There is an antidote."

I pulled a small vial out of the inner pocket of my jacket. Only two inches tall, it was filled with a crystal clear liquid.

"Right here. Just the one vial, I'm afraid. The antidote is rather difficult to make."

She tried to grab it from me, but I held it out to the side, threatening to shatter it on the stone table.

"Ah, ah. None of that. This poison is fast acting. The antidote must be delivered in a few minutes, or it's lethal. If I break this vial, even I couldn't get another dose for you in time."

Her teeth ground so hard together I was surprised they didn't crack.

"What do you want?"

"Here's what's going to happen." I stood from the table, keeping both my arms up so everyone could see the vial in my hand. "My bodyguards and I are going to leave. Once we've gotten to our car, I'll leave this vial behind. Then you're going to report to the Pahkan that we are looking into the theft of your shipment, and will tell you if we find anything. Deal?"

I started walking out of the room before she replied. She would agree. There was no choice. While she was certainly willing to die for her Pahkan and the Russian mafia, she obviously hated me due to my mixed heritage. Her pride wouldn't let me be the one to kill her.

Eva and Gavriil still had their guns

drawn when they met me at the door out of the room.

"Sir," Eva said through clenched teeth.

"Not now." My chest felt tight, and the words didn't come out as strongly as I wanted.

"But, sir," Gavriil whispered so low even I could barely hear him. "You're not immune to..."

"I'm aware. Keep walking."

For once, I wished my family's invention wasn't so efficient. By the time I reached the stairs leading to the lower level, my legs were already starting to go numb. I clung to the railing with a white-knuckled grip, forcing my feet to move one in front of the other. Aslanov's people were watching me. I had to remain calm and maintain the ruse that I was fine. If they knew I was dying as quickly as she was, I would lose my advantage.

Gavriil ran ahead of us to fetch the car and bring it right up to the front door of the museum. Just before I slipped inside the safety of the backseat, I smiled at Aslanov's people and set the vial of antidote on the curb for them to retrieve.

Then we drove away before they could try to stop us.

"Boss, quick. Take this." Eva shoved another antidote vial into my hands.

The liquid was bitter on my tongue, but tightness in my chest eased almost immediately.

"That was risky," she scolded while taking my pulse. "Another minute and it would have been too late. Even the antidote wouldn't have helped."

"Well, at least the Russians believed my lie about only having one vial. And we all got out of there unharmed."

I took too deep a breath and started coughing.

Eva handed me a handkerchief. "You call this unharmed?"

Dabbing at my mouth, I was glad to find no bloodstains on the white cloth. I'd taken the antidote in time. There was no damage to my lungs.

"Alive," I corrected myself. "At least we're all alive. And we have a chance to figure out what's going on before the Russians get really angry."

The car was filled with silence as we drove down the street away from the harbor. I regarded my bodyguards with a critical eye. They'd been with me for twenty years. Some things didn't need to be said.

But then again, some things did.

"I know the reason my Russian relatives gave you to me as bodyguards was so you would spy on me for them."

Both Eva and Gavriil opened their mouths to argue, but I cut them off.

"No, don't bother. I knew from the day I accepted you that you were a leash as much as a shield. I'd rather have you here, out in the open, than have you spying on me secretly. However, this means you must report to someone in the Russian mafia. I need you to use those contacts and find out everything you can about the incident fifteen years ago. Neither side was able to catch the thief, but maybe by combining information we can figure out who's responsible."

The pair were silent for a moment, communicating only with their eyes, before they came to a decision. Based on the expressions on their faces, it seemed to be a decision in my favor.

"We'll see what we can do," Gavriil said while still paying attention to the road. "Do you really think the thief from fifteen years ago is the same person who stole the recent shipment?"

"I don't know." I leaned back against the seat and closed my eyes, concentrating on taking deep even breaths as the antidote continued to do its work. "But Aslanov was right about one thing. Even if it's not the same person, it's still the same problem. The two incidents must be related somehow, and that might be the key to catching our thief."

CHAPTER TWELVE

D'Angelo

THE ERODANCE WAS classier than many similar places. There was a Las Vegas vibe to the club, with many flashing lights and everything styled to be just a little over the top. However, the guests weren't allowed within ten feet of the stage, and it was clear that effort had been put into keeping the dancers safe and comfortable.

I was a bit surprised when, upon entering, I was instructed to download the club's app. Apparently, instead of letting guests throw money at the dancers, tips were given through online transactions. It was a different way of doing things, but after only a few minutes, I could see the appeal.

Instead of worrying about collecting money on the spot directly from guests, the dancers could focus on performing more complex routines that seemed specially choreographed to highlight the best assets of each dancer. One routine showed off the flexibility and long legs of the man on the pole, while another was a display of the dancer's strength.

They were talented, but none of them were the dancer I most wanted to see, so I didn't pay much attention.

Since it was a gay club, Eva had stayed outside to guard the perimeter while Gavriil came in with me, loitering near enough to be in sight without actually crowding me. Maybe it was irresponsible, going out to a club so soon after my incident with the Russians, but the antidote had left me feeling slow and sluggish. I needed something to get my adrenaline up and my blood pumping, and this club held the perfect solution.

Just as I'd hoped, a few moments later the music changed and a familiar figure stepped out onto the stage. If I hadn't already known that Oliver worked here, I might not have recognized him. The mask was designed to match his outfit, and with a stage name like "Phantom" it seemed like a stylistic choice rather than one of necessity.

Every performance that night had a neon sci-fi theme, and Oliver was no exception. He swung himself up onto the pole as the opening notes of Katy Perry's *Extraterrestrial* started playing. His black leather outfit blended into the background, but the neon details stood out in contrast, creating an illusion that he was constantly flickering in and out of focus.

Like a whisper making someone listen harder in order to hear it, Oliver's outfit and movements also made people watch him closer.

Leaning back in my chair and sipping on my drink, a rather well made Old-fashioned, I enjoyed the show. Some people might feel jealous in such a situation, but I'd always liked letting others gawk and admire my riches. I liked the way other people's eyes burned when they gave into their covetous nature, and the bitter disappointment that overcame them when they realized they could never have the thing they desired.

Other people's hands, however, were a different matter. For the same reason I kept my valuables locked behind a glass display case, I never shared my lovers with anyone else.

I knew the club offered "private" services. The door to the back rooms stood beside the stage, unmarked but obvious in its purpose. However, I was also certain that Oliver had never participated in any private "dance". On our date, he'd kissed with passion but inexperience. He was obviously unused to the touch of other people.

Well, I wouldn't let it stay that way for long.

Oliver's performance was nearly half over when I noticed something strange. During our date, he had claimed that the burn on his face wasn't the only one, yet the body being displayed on stage looked flawless.

For a moment I questioned if I was actually watching the right person. However, as the dancer spun in a move that arched his back in a tantalizing display of flexibility, the stage lights glinted off his earring and I was once again certain that this person was Oliver.

His outfit included a pair of tall gloves that encased his entire arms but left his hands mostly uncovered so he could grasp the pole. It was possible that the other burns were only on his arms, yet his description seemed to imply the marks were on his body as well.

I would have to ask him about it later.

The song ended and Oliver finished his performance artfully draped over the stage floor. Years of conditioning in high-stress environments kept me calm on the outside, but on the inside my blood ran hot and my pants felt tighter than they had been a few minutes ago.

With the barest movements, I readjusted my clothes to lie more comfortably. Off to the side, Gavriil noticed my fidgeting and smirked.

After the performance, Oliver then climbed off the stage and mingled with the rest of the room. He laughed and flirted with guests, encouraging them to buy more drinks. It almost seemed genuine, but I'd been on the receiving end of his actual flirtations, and this was definitely an act.

I gave it a few minutes before finishing

off my drink and heading over to where Oliver was talking with another guest. At first, I didn't intend to interrupt and was content to wait until he was done. This was his job, after all. Interfering now would be just as inappropriate as if he interrupted my meeting with the Russians.

That idea went out the window when I drew close enough to hear their conversation.

"What'd you mean *not available*?" the guest demanded as he stood close enough to Oliver for their sides to press together. "You're here. That means you're available."

Oliver tried to maneuver the man's hand off his shoulder, but it only slipped down to his hip. "As I said, I'm not available at the moment. But Echo and Lux should be free right now."

I slipped behind the pair, so far unnoticed as the man's hand gripped Oliver's hip tighter.

"I've already signed up for the stupid app and paid the cover fee to get in here. You owe me a dance."

With a practiced move, the smile never left Oliver's face as he pinched the back of the man's hand to remove it. "Private dances have their own charge, and I don't owe you anything. We have plenty of other dancers who are available for private shows. One of them would work better for you."

Thick fingers gripped onto Oliver's wrist, and my patience reached its limit. "Listen here—" the man started to say, but he never finished his statement.

I grabbed his wrist, pressing on a pressure point that forced him to let go, while my other arm curled over Oliver's shoulders. "I'm afraid you're too slow. I've already snagged this one for myself. You'll have to find someone else to entertain you."

The man looked like he was about to argue, but I squeezed his wrist harder until he flinched from the pain and his whole arm buckled. "Fine," he said and snatched his wrist out of my grip. "Too much trouble anyway."

I let him leave without a fight, preferring to give my attention to Oliver instead.

Wide hazel eyes stared up at me in shock, evident even through the half-mask covering his face.

Taking advantage of his shock, I guided him over to the door leading to the back rooms. It was surprisingly easy to gain access once I submitted the necessary payment through the club's app. I tossed a look toward Gavriil, silently ordering him to stay and keep guard in the main room, then disappeared with Oliver through the door.

When we were finally alone in one of the private rooms, Oliver snapped out of his stupor.

"What are you doing here?"

Giving him my most disarming grin, I took a seat in the plush, padded armchair positioned right in front of a small stage. "What'd you mean? I'm a customer, just like anyone else."

I watched the wheels turn in Oliver's eyes as he wondered if I recognized him. For a moment, I debated keeping up the ruse and watching him squirm, but his real personality was so much better than the act he put on for guests.

"Don't look so worried, Oliver. I know who you are."

His shoulders slumped in a mix of relief and resignation. "Oh. How, um, how did you recognize me?"

I took a moment to admire him from head to toe, letting my gaze drag along his body longer than necessary. "Between the mask and the jewelry, it's rather obvious."

Oliver's hands shot up to his earrings, which resembled a pair of planets with spinning rings. "My jewelry?"

"Yeah. You're still wearing jewelry made by your friend. Like I said before, it's distinctive. What are the odds someone wearing only this specific brand of jewelry would also include a mask in their costume that covers the whole left side of their face?"

Rather than reassure him, my answer only seemed to make him more nervous. He chewed on his thumbnail as a whole new wave of worries crashed over him. "Right. That makes sense. Uh, sorry. It must have been a shock to come in here and see me like this. You aren't mad, are you?"

Should I tell him that I already knew about his night job when I came here?

In fact, his presence was the very reason for my visit?

No.

There was no way to explain how I knew without revealing the background search I'd done on him. Such things were standard in the world I lived in, but to an ordinary civilian, it would seem invasive and suspicious.

Waving him over, I invited him to join me. He sat delicately on the arm of the chair, still obviously nervous about my reaction.

"Mad?" My hand settled on his bare leg. "Why would I be mad? You're a joy to watch. I'm not going to complain about such an opportunity."

I trailed my hand up his leg, enjoying the feel of his smooth skin, until my fingers were high enough to tug at a strap of his costume.

Oliver didn't even seem to notice my touch, too distracted by his own fretting. "You really don't mind? Ashes is the only one who knows about this job. I haven't even told my family. They'd be horrified. I'd understand if you're disgusted with me."

I snapped the strap of his costume to get his attention.

He yelped at the unexpected sting against his skin, but obviously wasn't hurt as he pouted at me.

"I am certain," I said as I soothed the

skin on his hip. "I think I already know the answer... but, are these "private dances" something you do regularly?"

"What? No." He shook his head so hard he nearly fell off the arm of the chair, giving me a perfect excuse to wrap both hands around his hips. "I've never taken a private client. The money was tempting, but I could never bring myself to..." He trailed off, looking around the intimate atmosphere of the private room like he was seeing it for the first time. "Wait a minute. How are we here?"

"I brought us here."

"No, I mean..." His startled expression turned back to me. "You have to pay to even access these rooms. You can't just walk in."

"Yeah." I waggled my phone in front of his face, showing the club's app open on the screen. "The app definitely makes it easy. More clubs should use this system."

He snatched the phone out of my hands and stared at the screen with his mouth hanging open. "This says... Do you really pay this much?"

"Not enough?" Taking my phone back, I stored it in the pocket of my jacket. "There wasn't a required amount, so I just paid what seemed like a good number."

He fisted his hands in the lapel of my jacket and pulled me closer like he was on the verge of both strangling me and kissing me. "That's twice as much as I've ever been offered."

If he expected me to be shocked, he was about to be let down. I merely laughed and tugged him closer so he was sitting properly in my lap. "Only twice? I'm not as impressive as I thought. Maybe I should add more."

In this position, my hands were free to wander over the rest of his body. So much skin lay vulnerable to my touch, but I started by removing his mask to expose his whole face.

"That's better. Much better than your "Phantom" persona. Although the stage name was a good choice." As I tossed the mask aside, I was reminded of another question I'd had earlier. "Hey. Feel free not to answer, but the other day you mentioned that the scar on your face wasn't the only one. Yet, this outfit shows off pretty much everything and..."

I let the rest of the question go unsaid. There was no good word choice available. If I said the rest of his skin looked flawless, that would imply I considered his scars to be a flaw.

He hesitated, chewing at his bottom lip as he no doubt chewed over his options. The sight was too tempting, and I pulled him forward into a kiss and ran my tongue over that tortured lip. With a gasp, he clung to me and eagerly returned the kiss with equal force. Several minutes passed before we parted, and he was left just as flushed and panting as he'd been after his performance earlier.

"I suppose I should show you," he said, though he couldn't meet my eye. "You'll see it eventually."

In one swift move, he tore off his left glove, revealing his bare arm. Just as I'd suspected, scar tissue intertwined with healthy pale skin, making the top half of his arm look like it was made of patchwork. These scars weren't as intense as the one on his face. The skin wasn't as distorted, but the burns covered a large area and had still probably been difficult to heal.

Without hesitation, I stroked my hand along his arm and mapped out the different textures of his skin. "Is it just these?"

He shook his head but didn't say a word. Instead, he dragged my hand over to his chest so my palm rested against his left pectoral.

I couldn't tell what I was feeling. The skin here looked fine, but it felt different. Smoother, and cooler than the skin in other areas.

"The gloves and the mask are easy to work into my costume," he said when I gave him a confused look. "But there's no good way to cover my chest. The whole point of this job is showing off as much skin as possible. So, instead, I use a silicone patch here. It looks just like skin, and it holds up to vigorous movement. I'll show you if you really want, but it's glued down and it's hard to get off. So..."

I patted his chest, right over his heart. "Leave it for now. As you said, I'll see it eventually." Looking him over again, I added all his scars together. "Everything is on one side. Let me guess. You were carrying your brother in your right arm and used your left to shield against the fire."

"I think so. To be honest, I don't really remember it very well. My body just, kinda, acted on autopilot. I don't remember making any decisions. I wasn't even certain what had happened until I woke up again in the hospital." He shook his head and his bangs fell over his face. "Let's not talk about it. You paid so much. That must mean you want a private dance. Right?"

If Oliver were a stranger, I would have agreed in a heartbeat, but I knew better than to sacrifice future prospects for momentary pleasure. I never would have lasted long in my position if I was that impulsive.

Brushing his bangs out of his face, I pressed a kiss to his cheek. "I certainly wouldn't say no to such an offer, but only if you want to. Paying to bring you back here was only to get you away from that handsy customer. I don't want you to feel like I'm trying to buy you. That never works well."

I'd fallen into that trap in the past, thinking I could buy someone's loyalty with money. It could work, for a time, but they were always the first to betray me.

To Oliver's credit, he actually did think about it for a moment, before coming to a decision. It made me feel more confident that the decision was his own, and not just something done to appeal to me.

"So, you're saying we can do whatever I want?" he asked, this time looking up at me through his eyelashes.

My answer came easily. "Just name it."

"Hmmm." He shifted around, and I thought he was going to leave, but instead, he merely moved so he was straddling my lap rather than sitting sideways. "Then, I think I want to stay right here."

His hands gripped either side of my head and he kissed me. While his inexperience still showed, the few kisses we'd exchanged so far had already helped him improve. There was no more awkward bumping of noses, and his tongue pushed its way into my mouth with some confidence. I let him lead the kiss for a few moments, but I refused to stay passive for long.

While he was distracted kissing me, my hands wandered down his body until I found the strap of his costume again. I snapped it, reveling in the sound of elastic against skin.

Oliver yelped into the kiss, and I could feel him shudder.

Gripping his chin in one hand, I forced

his head back enough so I could look into his eyes. "Seems like you enjoyed that." I snapped the strap again and watched as his pupils dilated. "Oh, yes. Definitely enjoying that. We'll have to play with that later. For now..."

I slipped my hand inside his costume and cupped him between his legs. I wasn't even moving yet, but my touch was still enough to leave him moaning and clinging to my shoulders like I'd already defiled him.

"You are going to be so much fun," I whispered before trailing a line of teasing kisses down his throat. "But for now, I'll keep it simple."

His costume ended up on the floor, so he was mostly naked in my lap as I stroked him to full arousal. The noises he made reminded me of a twittering bird as his hips twitched and jerked with each stroke of my hand. It seemed like he might be trying to grind against me, the same way he practically made love to the pole when he danced. For someone who could move so erotically on stage, he lost all sense of coordination the moment he tried to do something for real.

My lips found the juncture of his neck,

and I sucked a deep bruise into the skin while at the same time I started moving my hand faster. His cock throbbed against my palm and I knew he was close. Just a little more and he would sing for me.

His fingers dug into my shoulders hard enough to leave marks as he came, his hot seed dribbling over my fist. White teeth bit into petal pink lips as he tried to keep himself silent. I kissed him, tasting his final moans as he shuddered through the last of his orgasm.

When he finished, he collapsed against my chest, panting heavily. He clung like a little octopus, arms and legs tangled around me like he was afraid I might disappear. It was a more needy gesture than I was used to from my lovers, but I found I didn't mind it. There weren't many people who trusted me so openly, and I was determined to enjoy it while I could.

Sitting back in the chair, I stroked a hand up and down his spine as I waited for him to recover. The private room was booked for at least another hour. We wouldn't be going all the way tonight, but an hour still provided plenty of opportunity to play with him a few more times.

CHAPTER THIRTEEN

Oliver

MY ALARM WENT off in the morning, but I didn't immediately jump out of bed. This was normal, as I was usually sluggish the morning after a shift at the club due to the lack of sleep. However, that morning I felt lighter, like I was floating just a few inches above my body, and I lay in bed savoring the sensation. Even just thinking about the previous night put a smile on my face and left my skin tingling all over.

D'Angelo and I hadn't even gone all the way, and I already felt like my brain had been replaced with marshmallow fluff. At this rate, actual sex would turn me into a useless puddle.

Eventually, about fifteen minutes later than usual, I rolled out of bed. Downstairs, Nana was on the phone with someone, and my mother was already in the kitchen putting breakfast together. I grabbed a place and started eating, while simultaneously packing the leftover sausage and eggs into a container for lunch.

My mother sat on the other side of the table, but rather than focus on her breakfast, she instead just stared at me.

"Rowan was telling me about your outing the other day. He said your date was, and I quote 'Giving off strong *Daddy* energy'. I'm not actually sure what that means, but the way he said it sounds like a good thing."

I choked on my breakfast and slapped myself on the chest to convince the eggs to stay out of my lungs.

"I wouldn't describe him like that. I mean, he's attractive, but..." I quickly stopped talking before I said anything more embarrassing.

Mother only grinned and poked at the fruit slices on her plate. "There's nothing to be embarrassed about. I'm just glad you're getting out there and meeting people. But you can't leave me in suspense. Tell me you at least have a picture for me to see."

I didn't say anything, but with a blush and a small smile I nodded and handed her my phone. There weren't many pictures of D'Angelo on there. Just one candid shot I'd managed to snap of him in the coffee shop, and a single picture from our date.

She studied the pictures for a moment, the thoughts behind her eyes unreadable. Although I was twenty-two, I still felt like a child waiting for my parent's approval.

"He does look just like Rowan described," she finally said. "Although... How old is he?"

Nervously clearing my throat, I swirled the orange juice in my glass until it made a whirlpool just so I wouldn't have to look at her directly.

"He's, um, thirty-eight."

Before Mother could say anything, Rowan rolled into the room. "Yeah. Oliver snagged himself a sugar daddy."

When I was younger I would have chucked a bread roll at his head. Although no longer a kid, I was still tempted.

"Shut up. It's not like that."

At the table, Rowan slid a plate closer to himself, but never stopped grinning at me. "Older. Rich. Obviously horny for your ass. Sounds like a sugar daddy to me."

I gave in to the childish impulse and actually did throw a roll at him. "You're a terrible brother. Making me sound like a gold-digger. I don't care about his money."

"What's this about money?"

I hadn't noticed Nana enter the room, and immediately fell silent as she approached the table.

"Take a look, Nana," Mother said as she handed over my phone. "We're talking about Oliver's date. He's handsome, isn't he?"

My phone, with its cracked screen and protective case printed with Van Gogh's *Starry Night*, looked odd in her hands. Somehow both too modern and too old at the same time. I had no idea how she would react to D'Angelo. She'd never had anything to say about my dating life before, but there also hadn't been much to talk about.

She was silent for a lot longer than I

expected, and I began to squirm nervously in my seat.

"Hmm," she eventually said, her lips pursing so tightly that the wrinkles around her mouth pulled smooth. "Not a good man."

"Nana," Mother scolded and snatched my phone back from her. "How can you say that about someone after just looking at a picture? Rowan says he was a real gentleman on their date. It was even his idea to bring Rowan in the first place."

"Yeah," Rowan agreed. "He was actually really nice."

Nana just sniffed with a look of obvious disdain. "Too old for Oliver. What is he? Twice your age?"

"Not that much," I mumbled, although as I did the math I realized she was almost right. Thirty-eight was only a few years away from being double my own age. However, D'Angelo looked younger than he really was, and unless Nana had been eavesdropping on my conversation with my Mother, then she shouldn't know his actual age.

Why should it matter anyway?

Would dating someone my own age who treated me like crap be better just because their years matched mine?

My appearance meant I had a more limited dating pool than most. I couldn't afford to be picky over something as pointless as age.

If Nana heard me, she gave no indication and just kept talking. "There's no good reason for an older man to pay attention to a boy your age. Your father would be horrified to know his son was involved with a man like this."

Silence descended over the table.

I stood from my seat without even realizing I'd moved. With numb hands, I took my phone back from my Mother, gripping it so tightly it was in danger of cracking again.

"Well, that's too bad. My father doesn't get a say in my love life since he ran off rather than deal with having a disabled son and an ugly one."

A guardian angel must have been looking out for me, because before I could say anything else, the alarm on my phone went off, warning me it was time to leave for work.

I stormed out of the house, so mad my blood felt like it was boiling in my veins, and slammed the door behind me.

CHASING DANGER

My rage still hadn't subsided by the time I boarded the public bus, and the dark look on my face ensured that I easily found a seat for myself. Grumbling under my breath, I sat down, clutched my backpack to my chest, and leaned my forehead against the cool glass.

Why did she have to bring up my father?

Even so many years later, the memory of him was still as sore as a fresh bruise.

It might not hurt so bad if he'd always been a terrible father, but the first years of my life were actually filled with happy memories. He wasn't the most present parent. He was often busy with work, so I didn't see him as often as I would like, but when he was home he acted like a proper father should. Helping me with homework, teaching me how to play catch, and that kind of cliché father-son stuff.

Mother also hadn't worked so much back then as well, so I had plenty of her attention whenever Father wasn't around.

All in all it had been a normal, happy childhood.

For the first seven years.

Everything seemed to unravel when

Rowan was born.

No, it was before that. Even before Rowan was born, when Mother was still pregnant, Father started acting even more distant than usual. It was like he knew something bad was coming, and he already had one foot out the door. When Rowan was born with SMA, it seemed to be the last nail in a coffin I hadn't even realized we were building. Then the house fire buried that coffin six feet under so it would never be seen again.

"Stupid Bastard," I muttered against the window as I watched the familiar streets roll by. A light summer rain dotted the glass with small drops of water and turned everything a milky gray color. "You can't just leave when things get hard."

CHAPTER FOURTEEN

Oliver

CREATING DESIGNS ON top of hot chocolate was harder than on a latte, since whipped cream didn't behave the same as milk foam, but I did my best. The little girl standing before the counter of the coffee shop wanted a fairy on her drink, and I was determined to deliver a fairy.

The end result wasn't perfect. One wing was bigger than the other and the leaf I wanted the fairy to be standing on looked more like a surfboard, but the little girl didn't seem to care as she squealed in delight all the same. Her tired looking mother flashed me a grateful smile and stuffed a few extra dollars in my tip jar.

All in all, it hadn't been a bad day. We'd been busy, thanks to the drizzly weather, but none of the customers had been too difficult, and I welcomed the distraction. Focusing on making coffee, and keeping track of any "green" orders that came through, stopped me from thinking too much about the conversation at breakfast.

There was an hour left in my shift, and I wasn't scheduled to work at the club tonight. If I was lucky, I might be able to swing by Ashes' place tonight for a combination of ranting and bragging.

Ranting about my Grandmother, and bragging about my night with D'Angelo.

The bell above the door rang, and I looked up to see a pair of men walk in. At first glance, they looked like standard businessmen. Not the most successful based on the fit of their suits—definitely off the rack rather than tailored—but they did well enough for themselves to walk with confidence. I would have completely overlooked them, but something nagged at my brain. A deeply buried instinct screamed words I couldn't understand, but it put me on alert.

The men ordered a pair of basic black coffees. No cream, no sugar, and no opportunities to have any fun. I was determined to get them their drinks and send them on their way as soon as possible.

I'd just finished the first drink when the bell over the door rang again. The mother and daughter left, pulling up the hoods of their jackets as they stepped out into the rain. At first the cute sight made me smile, until I realized that I was left alone with the two strange men.

I handed the first man his drink and was about to start on the second, when I finally realized what had caught my attention about them.

Their shoes were wrong.

There were a selection of shoes that could be worn with suits, but heavy black boots that laced up above the ankle weren't on that list. No self-respecting businessman would be caught dead wearing such shoes. These were the shoes of a laborer. Someone who wasn't afraid to get dirty, and needed footwear that could keep up with their rugged lifestyle.

I realized I was staring and quickly

looked away, turning back to the coffee machine to finish the second drink.

I was thinking too much. They were just shoes. An odd choice of shoes, yes. But at the end of the day, just shoes. Maybe there was a special reason they needed that kind of footwear. All I needed to do was give them their drinks and stop worrying so much.

"Busy day?" the first man asked, swirling his coffee in the cup without actually taking a sip. "Isn't it hard to handle this place on your own?"

The coffee machine made a loud beep as it finished filling the cup. "My co-worker is around here somewhere cleaning up. We're closing in less than an hour."

That was a lie. I was scheduled to close the shop on my own, like I was every night I worked the closing shift, but they didn't need to know that.

Placing a lid on the second cup, I turned around to hand off the drink, only to feel something hard and metal pressing into my chest. I'd never seen a gun up close before, and it took me a moment to realize what was in front of me.

The cup slipped from my hand, spilling

plain black coffee all over the floor. "Sir, what..."

The bell rang again as several more people stepped into the shop. The last one locked the door, and like a coordinated unit, they started closing the blinds over each floor length window.

It was probably a dumb idea, since there was a gun pointed right at my chest, but the moment I saw them start closing the blinds I panicked and bolted for the shop's backroom. There was a back door through the supply cupboard that I might be able to escape through.

I didn't even make it through the swinging door into the back room, let alone the storage closet. I barely took more than a few steps before one of the men with the wrong shoes vaulted over the counter and grabbed me around the waist.

"Now, now. None of that. Just cooperate quietly and you'll be fine."

He lifted me up by my waist so my feet dangled in the air. I struggled, but with nothing to brace against I felt like a piece of wet laundry flapping on the drying line.

"The money's in the till. Just take whatever you want and leave me alone."

One of the men scoffed, but from my position I couldn't tell which one.

"Pfah. We're not here for your petty cash. Now quiet down."

I whimpered but bit my lip to keep from making sound as I was dragged back over to the group. One of the men, at that point they all looked the same to me, grabbed me by the chin and forced me to look up at him.

"You sure this is the right one?"

"Yeah." The man holding me let me go, but kicked the back of my knee so I collapsed to the floor. "Has to be this one, unless this place just so happens to have another barista with a half-melted face."

Some of the men laughed.

I was too terrified to care about the insult. I'd certainly been called worse.

"But, really, why this one?" the man with all the questions kept asking. "Can't even sell him with a face like that. Seems like a waste of effort."

"Hey," the first man, who seemed to be in charge, smacked the questioning man over the back of the head. "We were paid to do a job. So shut up, and do your job."

"Yeah, yeah," the questioning man grumbled and rubbed the back of his head. "You guys get the brat loaded up. The rest of us will prep the location so we can torch it on the way out."

Two men grabbed me under the arms and dragged me to my feet. They started pulling me toward the back room. I'd tried to run there myself a moment ago, but now my route to freedom felt more like a death row march.

"No, wait, stop," I shouted and dug my heels into the floor. "There must be a mistake. Who even are you?"

"Ugh," one of the men groaned. "Will someone shut him up?"

Without warning, a large palm slapped me across my cheek. The blow left my ears ringing and everything turned sideways for a moment. I barely even felt the pain. Everything was happening too fast to keep up; my brain seemed to be shutting down.

One of the men suddenly let out a strange little shout. He stood frozen, looking down at his chest where his white shirt had turned red. Everyone stared at him in confusion for a moment, before he dropped to the floor like a lifeless ragdoll.

"What the hell?" one of the men holding me shouted.

There was a faint clink of breaking glass, before another man collapsed. He fell face up, and I could see a small hole in his forehead that was oozing red in thick streams over his face.

I felt faint, and my breath came in quick frenzied gasps.

"Quick, get away from the windows," one of the men shouted.

Everyone scattered to press their backs against the walls or duck behind tables, while one man forced me down behind the counter. I could no longer see what was going on, only hear their panicked voices.

"We closed the blinds."

"How the hell are they shooting us through the window?"

The familiar sound of the greeting bell was accompanied by the unfamiliar sound of the front door being smashed off its hinges. Someone else had broken into the shop, and the situation on the other side of the counter turned to chaos.

I slapped my hands over my ears and prayed for it to end. Whatever was happening, it had nothing to do with me. I wanted no part in it.

The people keeping me behind the

counter eventually left to join what must have been some sort of fight.

I was alone. Unguarded. I could run. I should run.

But, they'd been trying to pull me out through the back door, so that way probably wasn't safe. The only other option was the front door.

Gripping the counter with shaking hands, I pulled myself up just enough to peer over the edge. As I'd guessed, it was a fight. Most of my attackers lay unmoving on the floor, their bodies sprawled like discarded rags. Only one man remained, and he stood just in front of the counter with a gun in hand, pointing the weapon directly at... D'Angelo?

My lover from last night was barely recognizable now. He still looked sleek and well put together, but there was a lethal edge to his demeanor, and a look in his blue eyes that reminded me of a wild beast trapped in a cage.

The man with the gun was shouting at D'Angelo.

"What the hell? You weren't supposed to be here!"

I didn't hear D'Angelo's response. My

gaze was locked on the man with the gun. This was the same one who had slapped me. The pain still burned in my cheek. My unscarred cheek. He'd struck that side on purpose, trying to ruin what remained of my original face and leave me nothing but scars.

Fury grabbed hold of me, calming my nerves in an unnatural icy bath of cold certainty. I wanted this man to suffer.

Before I realized what I was doing, I picked up the coffee pot and, with an inhuman yell, I smashed it over the man's head. Glass shattered, and hot coffee poured out over his face and scalded his skin. The man didn't have time to make a single noise before he collapsed.

Maybe he was unconscious. Maybe he was dead. I didn't know, and at that moment I didn't care. All I felt was relief that he couldn't hurt me again.

"Oliver?" D'Angelo said carefully, holding his hands out as he approached me like he was trying to sooth a feral animal.

The calm I'd felt when I picked up the coffee pot disappeared quicker than a popped balloon. I started shaking again, even worse than before.

Looking down at my hand that still held the coffee pot handle, I realized my vision was going blurry.

"I think I'm going to sit down now."

Then my vision went black as I fainted.

CHAPTER FIFTEEN

D'Angelo

THERE WERE SEVERAL instances in my life that made me want to take up smoking. It was a disgusting habit of my father's, and I had no actual interest in it, but the promise of calming my nerves was tempting.

Sitting by the side of my own bed, waiting for Oliver to wake up, was one of those moments.

A doctor on my payroll had already checked him out to be sure Oliver hadn't been poisoned or injured. Apparently, he'd just passed out from the combination of extreme stress and lack of sleep. He worked late night shifts at the Erodance, then had to get up early for his coffee shop shift. It wasn't ideal, but there shouldn't be any negative effects.

So, now it was just a matter of waiting for him to wake up naturally.

As the minutes ticked by, slowly turning into hours, I sat watching the shadows move along the walls. A knife twirled through my fingers, flashing its deadly edge back and forth. It was a nervous habit I'd picked up almost as soon as I learned to wield a knife properly. Not only did it help me retain a sense of control in uncertain situations, but it also worked as a decent intimidation tactic.

In this case, I didn't want to scare Oliver, and made a note to sheath the knife back in the hidden strap on my wrist as soon as he woke up. He was likely going to be overwhelmed and didn't need to see me looming over him holding a weapon as soon as he opened his eyes.

As much as I wanted him to wake up, I also wanted him to sleep longer. The moment he returned to consciousness I would have to explain what happened to him.

What would I even say?

Oliver was a civilian. I knew that, for our relationship to continue, I'd eventually have to tell him about my position in the mafia and the dangers that came with it. However, I'd been planning on having a little more time before bringing it up.

Oliver stirred, twisting his fists in the sheets, and burying his face against the pillow.

I sat up straight and stored my knife back in its sheath.

Hazel eyes opened and stared at me with bleary focus. At first, he smiled, and warmth filled the hollow place in my chest. But then his gaze focused, and his memories seemed to return to him. He sat up abruptly, half tangled in the sheets, and scrambled away until his back hit the wall.

"D'Angelo. What the hell?"

I sighed and ran my hands through my hair. "You're going to need to be more specific."

He started talking, but his voice failed before he finished forming the first word. Several more attempts ended in the same result, until eventually, he gave up talking and just hid his face in his hands. Curled up with his knees drawn to his chest, he looked like a confused little ball of misery.

I wanted to reach out to him, but I didn't know how it would be received, so I just sat quietly and waited.

"Did that actually happen?" he eventually asked without looking up. "I smashed a coffee pot on someone's head."

I nodded, then realized he couldn't see me while he was still staring at his knees. "It was a very effective tactic."

Oliver finally did look up, his expression both fearful and angry. "It wasn't a tactic. I panicked. A bunch of guys attacked the coffee shop and tried to kidnap me. And then you showed up and... I don't even know what you did."

Despite everything he said, none of it was a question, so I didn't know what to answer.

In the end, I didn't need to say anything. Oliver regained his composure surprisingly quickly and sharp clarity returned to his eyes as his thoughts worked double-time piecing things together.

"You weren't surprised then, and you don't look surprised now. It's like you already knew what was happening and what to do."

Those hazel eyes, which were usually so warm, narrowed like the lens of a microscope, pinning me under observation.

"What's going on? You obviously know, so just tell me."

He was either exceptionally brave or hadn't fully processed what he was saying. There were very few people who dared to demand answers from me. Even my past lovers weren't usually so bold. I was unused to it, but seeing such audacity coming from Oliver... Well, I didn't hate it.

"I'm not certain who attacked you." He started to protest, but I stopped him. "I have a few ideas. I just can't say which of my enemies are responsible."

"Your enemies?"

Although he'd made his first deductions with such confidence, now that I'd agreed with him, he couldn't seem to believe it. "Why do you have enemies like that? Why would they attack me? That doesn't make sense. You're not telling me something. Wait..." He looked around, noticing the unfamiliar bedroom he was lying in for the first time.

"Where am I? Did you... did you kidnap me?"

"Kidnap is a strong word. You were unconscious, so I brought you back to my place." I gestured out the window at the view outside. We were in a penthouse on the edge of the city, so the Baltimore skyline stood tall against the cloudy night sky. "Or, at least the place I'm renting while I'm staying here in Baltimore. It's only temporary."

Oliver stared at the window like he was considering jumping out of it, but we were twenty-eight floors up and that particular window didn't open, so I wasn't worried. Surprisingly, this was a conversation I hadn't experienced very often. Most people that needed to know who I was were already in the know, and I rarely needed to explain.

The words didn't come easily.

I was saved from further questions by a knock on the door. A moment later, Gavriil poked his head inside.

"Boss. Alex Mariano has called several times. He wants an update about the situation."

As much as I wanted to tell Alex to fuck off right now, the Mariano family was not an enemy I could afford to make.

"Tell him I'm figuring it out and I'll let him know when I have answers. Just lay low for the time being."

With a sharp nod, Gavriil disappeared, and I was once again left under the full scrutiny of Oliver's suspicious gaze.

"Boss?" he repeated the word, turning it into a question. "Is he your employee?"

I could have lied, but then what?

One lie would lead to another and another. Once I went down that road there was no going back until it reached its inevitable disastrous end. That wasn't what I wanted.

"He's one of my bodyguards."

Bodyguard," Oliver repeated. "Why do you need a bodyguard? No, wait... go back. Why was I attacked... Oh, God. My family. Are they safe? What if they were attacked, too?"

He jumped up from the bed, tripping over the sheets tangled around his legs and nearly slamming his face into the bedpost.

Shooting out of my chair, I managed to catch him before he injured himself. "Whoa. Calm down. Everything's fine."

"Fine?" he shouted, though the close

call seemed to have shaken him enough that he easily followed my guidance and sat back down. "This is not fine. This is the exact opposite of fine."

"I just meant that your family is safe. I've put a protection detail on them and can move them to a safe house if necessary. Your friend as well. Everyone is safe."

Running a hand over his face, Oliver mumbled into the palm of his hand. "Protection details. Safe houses. Just like that." He breathed deep for a few moments as I sat back down in the nearest chair and waited.

It didn't take as long as I expected for him to finally lower his hand and look me in the eye with a determined gaze.

"Who are you? Normal people don't have bodyguards and safe houses on standby. Not to mention the room full of armed men that you took out single handedly. I'm not stupid. Something is going on and I want to know. I deserve that much after I've been dragged into the middle of it."

"You're right," I said, and he seemed startled by my quick agreement. "You deserve to know. Just... bear with me. I don't often have to explain this."

I started at the beginning, explaining my mix of Russian and Italian heritage. How I inherited leadership of one of the most powerful Italian mafia families when I was only eighteen and maintained that position for twenty years through a mix of ruthless violence and cunning politics.

Oliver was oddly silent as he listened to me. He didn't say a word. He barely even blinked as he absorbed everything I said like a dry sponge that had suddenly found itself submerged under far more water than it could hold.

It was only as I explained recent events that he began to fidget, pawing at his hair to pull it in front of his face. I recognized it as a nervous gesture whenever he was feeling self-conscious, so I wrapped up my explanation quickly.

It was probably either the Russians or Caprice Vidales' people who attacked him, though I wasn't certain which one. No matter who it was, he was obviously in danger due to his association with me. So, he needed to stay here where it was safe while I sorted everything out.

When I'd finished, he still didn't say anything. By that point, he'd stopped staring at me and now sat on the edge of the bed staring out the window again.

"I didn't intend to get you involved," I said, just to fill the silence. "Originally, I just wanted a distraction to keep me entertained while I was in town. But then I realized that you wouldn't just fall into my bed. Winning you would require effort. I probably should have walked away at that point, but I liked the effort. It was refreshing."

Standing from my chair, I stepped around the bed and reached out to lay a hand on his shoulder, but he flinched away from my touch.

Not wanting to push him, I stepped back.

"It's my fault that you're in danger now, so I promise I'll protect you. Just stay here while I take care of this, and I'll get you back to your normal life as soon as I can."

I turned to leave, but at the last moment he grabbed the very edge of my sleeve.

"Thanks, I guess, for telling me... and for taking responsibility. I'm just... I don't know what I'm feeling right now. I'm not angry. I'm just... numb."

Gripping his hand in both of mine, I gave it a squeeze. "That's understandable. It's a lot to process. Take some time to think things over. I promise to take care of you, so I'll be gone for a little while. You have free rein of the penthouse. It's fully stocked so you shouldn't need anything. Just don't try to leave. I'm assigning a bodyguard to watch over you and they will stop you from leaving if necessary."

I pulled out a basic phone from my pocket, which I placed on the side table by the bed. "This is a secure phone. It'll only call the numbers already programmed. You can use it to reach me and check in on your family and your friend. If you do need anything, just ask Eva and she'll get it for you. I'll be back in two days."

He gave me a nod and a non-committal grunt of agreement, which I figured was probably the best I was going to get. Then I left him alone and closed the bedroom door behind me.

"Eva, you're staying here."

"But, Boss..." she started to argue.

"No, I don't trust anyone else to guard him. Not until I know for sure who attacked him in the first place. Gavriil will be with me, so I won't be alone, and I don't plan on getting into any trouble."

She crossed her arms and raised an eyebrow at me. "You never 'plan' for any trouble. It just happens. And the fact that we don't know who attacked that boy and what they want, means you're in more danger, too."

Heading for the front door, I grabbed my coat and swung it over my shoulders to protect me from the dreary weather outside. "Doesn't matter. You're staying. I should only be gone for two days. Make sure he stays here until I get back and get him anything he needs."

She agreed, but from the tone of her voice I could tell she hated being relegated to what she saw as 'babysitting duty.' Still, I had faith that she would follow my order to the letter, even if she didn't like it.

Gavriil followed right behind me as I left the penthouse and stepped out into the hallway toward the elevator. "Two days? So, we're leaving the city. You have a plan."

Pressing the button to call the elevator, I watched the numbers slowly count up to our floor. "It won't solve everything, but I think I know how to solve at least one of our problems."

The elevator dinged and the door opened, but rather than immediately step on, I flashed Gavriil a violent smile.

"We're going to visit The Wolf."

CHAPTER SIXTEEN

D'Angelo

I HEARD THE dripping sound before I even finished stepping through the door. It didn't fit with the fine atmosphere of the private rooftop terrace.

Las Vegas had no shortage of five-star restaurants, just as it had no shortage of citizens and tourists to fill them. At this time of day, such an expensive restaurant would usually be packed with rich clientele, along with those trying to pretend they were rich for a night.

Instead, it sat empty except for a single diner. Sitting at a pristine white table spread, with a lavish multi-course meal spread before him, was Nathan Sterling. He was busy staring at something off to the side of the terrace, and just out of my sight, but he looked toward me with a smile as I approached.

"D'Angelo. I was surprised when I got your call."

Despite the spread of food, there was no wait staff present. Instead, Nathan's personal security handled everything. A man dressed as strictly as a secret service agent pulled out a chair at Nathan's table, silently inviting me to sit.

"Renting out the entire restaurant to yourself. Isn't that a bit much, even for you?"

Nathan spread his hands before him, indicative of Jesus's pose from The Last Supper. However, there was nothing saintly about his expression, as he grinned wide enough to flash one particularly sharp canine.

"How else is a man supposed to work and eat at the same time?"

For the first time, I noticed what Nathan had been looking at earlier. Something large hung from the main rafters of the terrace, swaying slightly in the breeze that blew constantly at such a drastic height above the desert city. It was so wrapped up in ropes and torn cloth, I didn't even realize what it was at first.

It was a body, hanging upside down by its feet and dripping blood onto the floor. At first, I thought it might already be dead, but then it twitched and a muffled moan could be heard through the gag covering most of its face.

Still alive then.

Probably male based on the size, but even that wasn't a guarantee, and it was in such rough shape I couldn't tell the gender just by looking.

"You having some problems?" I asked Nathan.

Gesturing dismissively with his knife, he returned to his meal. "No. Just a rat poking its nose in where it doesn't belong. I didn't have pest control written into my schedule, so I had to take care of it during dinner. I hate working while enjoying a meal, but there was no choice. Business has to get done."

This was the reason Nathan was so feared by those who knew him. He was ruthless, but in a completely systematic way. Some people in positions like mine delighted in the violence and the brutality. Even I was guilty of this on occasion. Nathan, however, was as ruthless as they come, but completely emotionally untouched by it.

It made him highly efficient.

He would be one of the most renowned mafia leaders in the world, if anyone knew he existed. To most of the world, the name Nathan Sterling meant nothing. It wasn't even his real name, just a more English sounding persona he'd taken on in order to blend in better with the western world. It was an ingenious ploy. He was the head of the Chechen mafia, yet he could go anywhere and do anything without the risk of being recognized.

Even international law enforcement, who specified in catching people like myself and Nathan, had no idea who he was. They all thought his sibling was the leader, when, in fact, that man was merely a figurehead. Nathan was the true leader, and he did it all behind a curtain of anonymity.

There were some days I wished I had that same luxury.

Glancing once again at the body hanging just a few feet away, and the bloody sunset painting the sky behind it, I addressed Nathan with a straightforward tone.

"You seem busy, so I won't take up too much of your time. I have a favor to ask of you."

Tapping the silver edge of his knife against his plate, Nathan regarded me with intense hazel eyes. They were a similar color to Oliver's eyes, yet they looked nothing alike. Nathan may not be known by name, but there were plenty of rumors surrounding him. He was referred to merely as The Wolf. It was originally a reference to Chechen's national animal and the symbol on their insignia, but the moniker fit.

As I met those hazel eyes, I felt like I was staring down a predator.

After a moment, he put down his utensils and leaned back in his chair, taking a slow sip from the wine in his glass. "It must be important if you've come to me directly instead of just asking over the phone."

I'd dealt with Nathan a few times before, so I recognized his ploy. He never stated anything as a question. To him, questions were a sign of weakness. Instead, he always posed everything as a statement, hiding how much he did or didn't know, and letting the other person assume their own questions.

I knew better than to walk into that trap.

"I always show respect where it's due, and a face-to-face conversation is much more respectful. Besides, it's the city of sin." I waved at hand at the cityscape that stretched over the horizon behind us, glowing with a mix of gold and neon as the rapidly setting sun gave way to night. "Of course I'm going to come here if I have an excuse. I wish more of my business resided in the west."

Setting his drink down, Nathan's expression turned serious, and he steepled his fingers to regard me over them. "Your favor."

It still wasn't a question, but it was as close as he ever came to one.

I couldn't risk pushing him any further.

"Caprice Vidales. I need her gone."

It was difficult to get a rise out of Nathan, but not impossible. He raised an eyebrow at me, his expression turning incredulous. When he realized I was serious, he laughed, throwing his head back to reveal the tattoos running up his neck. He wore a high collared shirt, so I couldn't see them enough to actually tell what they were, only that they were numerous and meticulously placed.

"That is certainly a favor," he said when his laughter finally subsided. "I still owe you for helping me with that little incident in Bosnia, but I don't owe you that much."

Tugging at my cufflinks to feign disinterest while simultaneously checking the knife hidden up my sleeve, I refused to sweat under the fire of Nathan's stare. "I'm not asking you to kill her. That would just cause more problems. I just need someone to get her out of my hair for a while so I can deal with other things."

"Yes, I imagine the Russians are keeping you plenty busy."

I looked up at him, moving a little quicker than I meant to.

Of course, Nathan caught my slipup and smirked at the evidence of my surprise. "Don't be like that. Yes, I know about your dealings with the Russians. Neither of you is exactly... subtle. Besides, the Mariano boy is too new to his position. It's obvious he'd ask you for help the moment trouble arises."

"Alex is doing surprisingly well taking over for his father, considering how unexpectedly he was shoved into the position."

Nathan laughed again. Two in one conversation. I was on a roll today.

"I never thought the old bastard would die." Nathan picked up his knife and fork again but didn't resume his meal. "The so-called 'Mafia King' was too set in his ways. We needed some new blood to take his place, though we'll see if Alex has the makings of a real leader, but that's not an issue for now."

He tapped the pointed tip of his knife against his bottom lip as he thought, letting the sharp edge rest dangerously against his skin. "Now, Caprice Vidales. That is a different problem altogether. Bothering her enough to keep her distracted, but not enough to accidentally start an unwanted war between our organizations will be difficult."

I waited in silence, with only the distant sounds of the city and the faint moans coming from the hanging body to keep me company. Even Gavriil wasn't close enough for me to exchange a glance with. My bodyguard had been forced to stay by the rooftop entrance, leaving me to face Nathan alone.

It took longer than I expected for Nathan to come to a decision, though I shouldn't have been surprised. Keeping people guessing was another one of his talents.

"Fashion," he eventually declared, and at first I thought I'd heard him wrong. Chuckling in dark amusement over my confusion, he explained further. "The Vidales family is involved in the high-end fashion industry. It's a lucrative enterprise, with plenty of bored rich people willing to throw their money away. Plus, it provides opportunities for money laundering, or smuggling, or whatever else I may need."

The hanging body gave a particularly loud moan.

With a quick flick of the utensils in his hand, Nathan signaled his security to deal with the disruption. I kept my eyes turned toward Nathan as the security man approached the body. There was an unpleasantly wet sound, and then the moaning stopped. The hanging person was still alive. I could still faintly hear them breathing, but they were much quieter.

Nathan continued speaking as if the interruption never happened. "I've been thinking about getting into the fashion industry for a while now but didn't have the motivation to do so. If you don't want me attacking Caprice Vidales directly, then attacking her financial stability would be a good distraction. Should keep her 'out of your hair' as you say."

Standing from my chair, I nodded deeply toward him. "I'll leave the details to you. If you succeed, then I'll owe you a favor."

Once again, Nathan grinned wide enough to show off his unusually sharp canine teeth. *The Wolf* was definitely a fitting title for him.

"There's no 'if' about it. I will succeed, and you will owe me."

"And I always pay my debts," I assured him. "Now, I've taken enough of your time. Enjoy your meal."

With my head high and my shoulders straight, I left the rooftop terrace behind on even, unhurried steps. Just before the door closed behind me, I saw Nathan stand from his seat and head over to where the still alive body hung, the knife from his dinner utensils still clutched in his hand.

Then the screaming started.

The door closed, cutting me off from the rooftop, and I led Gavriil safely out of the building so we could head straight back to the airport.

I couldn't afford to leave Oliver alone for long.

CHAPTER SEVENTEEN

D'Angelo

KNOWING THAT CAPRICE would be taken care of for the moment was a weight off my mind, but I would have been happier with some evidence proving she was the one behind the attack on Oliver. Still, my hands were at least freed up enough to focus solely on the issue with the Russians.

Gavriil and Eva were still looking into the incident that started everything fifteen years ago. They were extremely efficient, not just as bodyguards, but also acquiring anything I demanded, so I expected them to have results shortly.

The prospect of finally having some answers left me in an optimistic mood as I approached the door to my temporary penthouse.

Maybe, now that Oliver had some time to come to terms with everything, we'd be able to talk properly.

My hand was on the knob, and I'd just cracked the door open when Gavriil grabbed my shoulder and stopped me.

"Hold on, Boss." He was looking at his phone, scowling over whatever he saw.

Before I could ask what the problem was, there came the unmistakable sound of a gun firing from inside the penthouse. Throwing off Gavriil's hand, I burst through the door, drawing my own gun to kill the intruder I expected to meet.

Instead, what I found was Oliver huddled against the wall, a bullet hole in the plaster just inches above his shoulder, and Eva standing over him holding a gun that was still smoking.

I saw red.

My feet barely made a sound on the carpeted floor, but there was no mistaking my violent intent as I charged at her.

"The hell are you doing?" I shouted as I

knocked the gun away. It went tumbling over the floor and was lost under the couch.

"Boss," Eva said, holding up both hands as if she were surrendering, but I knew her too well. Even without a weapon, she was still lethal.

Before she could say or do anything else, I swung at her, putting all my strength into the punch aimed right at her face. She had no choice but to step back or risk a broken jaw.

"Don't even try to deny what I just saw. You lied to me when you agreed to protect him. If I'd returned even a minute later, he'd be dead, killed by the very person I trusted to keep him safe." I grabbed my gun from the holster at my waist, aiming it at my former bodyguard, my finger poised to pull the trigger.

"Boss, wait." Gavriil grabbed my arm, trying to make me lower the gun.

Instinct took over and I swung at him with the butt of my gun. He dodged, putting distance between us, but this gave Eva an opportunity to snatch the gun from my hand.

In the ensuing tussle, my gun was lost as well, and we were left fighting barehanded.

Under ideal circumstances, I could probably hold my own against one of them. The two of them together against me, however, was an almost guaranteed loss.

So, it was a surprise when I managed to land a solid punch to Eva's gut, forcing her to double over. The body armor she wore under her clothes protected her ribs, and bruised my knuckles, so she wasn't injured, but she was winded.

Taking the opportunity, I grabbed Gavriil's wrist and twisted him around into a judo throw over my shoulder. He crashed into a table, snapping one of the legs with the crack of splintering wood.

Eva had just managed to right herself when I swept her legs out from under her. The carpet cushioned her fall but couldn't protect her when I climbed on top of her and pinned her to the floor. Unsheathing my knife from its hidden strap on my wrist, I pressed the blade to her throat just enough to break the first layer of skin without drawing blood.

Every muscle in my neck strained with furry, and I could barely unlock my jaw enough to speak as I looked down at her.

"Twenty years. Twenty years you've been at my side, and you choose now to betray me?"

The click of a gun cocking halted my hand. Eva and I had both lost our guns, but in the chaos, I'd forgotten that Gavriil was still armed. He knelt on the other side of the room among the splinters of the broken table with his gun held in one steady hand. The barrel pointed right at me, but his finger wasn't on the trigger yet.

"Boss, wait. It's not what you think."

Eva very slowly tapped me on the arm, careful not to move her head to avoid accidentally slitting her own throat on my knife. "We've been looking into things, like you said."

Without looking away from me, one of her hands slid along the floor until she pointed at Oliver, who was still huddled in a ball against the wall.

"He isn't who he says he is."

CHAPTER EIGHTEEN

Oliver

TWO DAYS PASSED in a fog. I left the penthouse's bedroom to get food from the kitchen occasionally, but I didn't remember eating anything. I spent my time either sleeping or reading one of the generic action novels stocked on the shelves. Anything to keep myself from thinking too much about my situation.

Not that I could ever really stop thinking about it.

A mafia boss.

My life had now officially entered "what the hell" territory. I wasn't even sure what I was supposed to think about the whole thing. The thought was too big. It wouldn't fit inside my head. Every time I tried, I found myself staring blankly at the wall for several hours.

Before I knew it, two days had passed, and the only thing I had accomplished was avoiding the bodyguard woman that D'Angelo had left behind. There was nothing wrong with her, but she practically radiated with an intense aura and watched my every move like an Olympic judge.

At least my family and Ashes were all right. I'd managed to talk to them through the cell phone D'Angelo left behind. The woman, Eva, had watched me extra closely during that conversation, making it clear that I wasn't meant to tell them anything about what was happening, but she didn't stop me. It turned out that my family and Ashes didn't even know there was anything wrong and that they were under protection. Apparently, D'Angelo's security detail were experts at doing their jobs secretly.

A knot inside me had loosened when I heard that. I'd been worried about causing stress for the people I cared about, but they thought D'Angelo had merely whisked me off for a spontaneous vacation. Ashes had even laughed while scolding me for moving so fast with my new beau.

Rowan had also been equally enthusiastic, though my Mother and Grandmother were oddly subdued. I couldn't really blame them. Leaving so suddenly, without warning, wasn't like me. They were probably worried about D'Angelo having too much influence on me and changing me into someone else.

I'd never dated anyone before, so they had no basis for comparison, plus the age gap added another concern to worry about.

If only that was my biggest problem,

My stomach growled. I realized I hadn't eaten anything since breakfast and the sun had almost set.

Pulling on a clean T-shirt—I didn't even want to ask how D'Angelo had clothing in my size—I slipped out the bedroom door and headed for the kitchen.

The first odd thing I noticed was that Eva seemed to be missing. She was probably somewhere else in the penthouse, it had several bedrooms after all, but over the last two days every time I set foot outside the master bedroom, she was always there, lurking in my peripheral.

Unnerved by the silence in the penthouse, I decided to just make some toast. Even the hum of the air-conditioner seemed too loud, and the sound of my own chewing was nearly unbearable. I hurried through the meal as quickly as I could and headed back to the master bedroom.

"Oliver Grant."

The unexpected sound of Eva's voice made me jump. With my heart beating out of my chest and my hand still on the bedroom doorknob, I turned around to face her.

"Yes. That's my name."

She was standing only a few feet away, somehow having approached without making a sound in the silent penthouse.

Her scowl deepened. "Are you sure?"

I gaped at her, searching her words for a hidden meaning I must have missed. "Am I sure... about my own name? Yeah, I think I am."

She took a step forward and I scurried away. Avoiding the confined space of the bedroom, I tried to move into the more open area of the front room.

"You say that so confidently," she said while she continued to approach. "But you're lying. Your name is Oliver Radcliffe."

I froze, though I couldn't help mouthing the name I hadn't heard in so many years. The syllables felt like I was running my tongue over barbed wire.

"How do you know that name?"

"Of course we looked into you. The name Radcliffe didn't come up at first, until we dug a little deeper. It was surprisingly well hidden. You almost got away with this little act."

"What act?" My back hit the wall on the far side of the front room. "What the hell are you talking about?"

She didn't even seem to hear me as she pulled the gun from her hip and pointed it at me. "Congratulations. In the twenty years I've been protecting D'Angelo, you came the closest to tricking me, but I won't let you hurt him."

I wish I could say I dodged the bullet intentionally, but when I saw the gun pointed at me, my fight or flight instincts both activated at the same time. One foot tried to run toward her for a confrontation, while the other tried to run away, and I just ended up tripping over my own legs. I hit the floor at the same moment the bullet hit the wall behind me.

Eva's gun immediately moved to point at me again, preparing for a second shot. I didn't even have time to try getting away.

A sudden bang made me curl up into a ball. For a moment, I was certain she had shot me, yet I felt no pain.

The noise continued, accompanied by shouting. With panic still burning like acid on my tongue, I dared to look up.

D'Angelo had appeared from seemingly nowhere, fighting with both of his bodyguards. At first, the sight of him filled me with cold fear, certain that he was trying to kill me as well, but then, I realized he was actually trying to stop them.

He was fighting to protect me.

Whatever had caused his bodyguard to attack me, it hadn't been on his order. In fact, if his shouting was anything to go by, the bodyguard had betrayed him.

D'Angelo and the two bodyguards eventually came to a stalemate, with him pinning Eva to the ground while the male bodyguard aimed a gun at D'Angelo.

A tense few seconds passed while nobody moved, until Eva slowly pointed at me.

"He isn't who he says he is. His name is actually..."

I shot to my feet. "Don't you dare. I threw that name away fifteen years ago. You have no right to bring it up again."

As I seethed, D'Angelo was busy staring between me and the two bodyguards, trying to come to a decision. Breathing deeply to resettle himself, he removed the knife from Eva's neck, but didn't put it back in its sheath.

"Oliver, stay there. You two, stand over there. Everyone's going to calm down and explain to me what the hell is going on."

The two bodyguards and I were put on opposite sides of the room, with D'Angelo standing in the middle. I couldn't tell who was protecting who at this point, but I didn't care. I just didn't want to hear that name again, but I had no way to stop them.

"We did a deeper background check on Oliver Grant, as you requested," Gavriil explained while Eva just nodded while rubbing her neck. "And some unexpected information came up."

An odd squawking sound escaped my mouth. I would have been embarrassed over the noise, but I was too distracted by my anger. "You ordered them to do a background check on me?"

D'Angelo wasn't nearly as ashamed by that fact as I thought he should be, meaning he wasn't ashamed at all. He just waved away that admission as if it were trivial. "I have background checks done on everyone I get involved with. It's necessary. More than one assassin has tried to kill me by worming their way into my bed."

"Right." I let the word drip off my lips, not sure what to do with it or what I should say next. "Fine. I understand... I guess. But that still doesn't explain why she tried to kill me."

Eva didn't answer me. In fact, she seemed to be pretending that I wasn't there. Instead, she spoke directly to D'Angelo.

"Boss, he's been lying to you. His name isn't Oliver Grant. It's Oliver Radcliffe. His father was Arturo Radcliffe."

As soon as that name left her mouth, hatred boiled up out of my stomach and spread through my veins like poison. My hand moved of its own accord, grabbing a book off a nearby shelf and throwing it across the room at her.

"Don't say that name. That bastard has nothing to do with me. He walked out on us right after the fire and I never heard from him again, so I never want to hear his name again, either. My Mom went back to her maiden name, and we got on much better pretending he didn't exist."

The book hadn't come close to hitting her. She didn't even have to move to avoid it, so nothing blocked her gaze when she finally looked at me. "That doesn't explain why your birth certificate was changed. Your father is listed as unknown."

"I don't know." I took a step across the room, as if to confront her, but then thought better of it and returned back to my safe place against the wall. "Like I said, we pretended like he didn't exist. My Mom probably had it changed so we could all forget about him."

"Hold on." D'Angelo stepped between us, blocking my line of sight to the pair of bodyguards so all I saw was his face in profile. He was obviously very confused. "Why are we arguing about this? I've never heard the name Arturo Radcliffe before. Why is it important?”

Very cautiously, like he was stepping onto thin ice, Gavriil approached D'Angelo and held out his phone. “You would never have dealt with him directly before, but he was a low-level enforcer for the Vidales family.”

“What?” D'Angelo snatched the phone from Gavriil's hands.

In contrast to D'Angelo's sudden burst of movement, I remained frozen.

“Who're the Vidales family?”

As D'Angelo scrolled through the information on the phone, he gave me a brief summary. The Italian mafia was not just one family, but several families arranged in a hierarchy. The Mariano family sat at the top, controlling everyone else, while the Bianchi family and the Vidales family held equal positions of power just below the top. Although part of the same organization, D'Angelo's family and the Vidales family were, in a way, rivals.

And apparently my father was a member of this hierarchy.

“No.” I shook my head wildly side to side. “No. My father worked at the harbor. He was a dock worker. He wasn't... He wasn't this." I gestured uselessly at D'Angelo, as if that would explain everything.

D'Angelo regarded me for a moment, then he held out the phone with a carefully neutral expression. "See for yourself."

With trembling hands, I took the phone. There, right on the screen, sat a picture of my father. He looked exactly as I remembered, and yet somehow completely different. His eyes were the same color as mine, and our noses were the same shape. His ears even stuck out a little like mine did. Yet, in the picture, he looked rough in a way I'd never seen before. A black eye along with several other cuts and bruises made him look like he'd just gotten out of a fight, and he glared directly at the camera. I was so shocked at first that I didn't immediately notice that the picture was a mugshot.

Listed below the picture was a horrifyingly impressive arrest record.

Drug dealing.

Larceny.

Multiple counts of every type of assault charge possible.

Attempted homicide.

Kidnapping?
Manslaughter?
I stopped reading after that.

"No, this isn't..." I sank to my knees and the phone tumbled from my hands, bouncing off the carpet. "This can't be."

A pair of perfectly polished shoes stepped into my vision before D'Angelo knelt down to look me in the eye. "I know it's a lot to take in, but the information is true. I'd have no reason to lie to you about this, and neither do they. If anything, I wish it wasn't true." He picked up the phone, turning the black rectangle over in his hands. "This isn't the kind of thing anyone should just have sprung on them... Wait a minute..."

He stood so abruptly that a breeze brushed over my skin in the wake of his movement. Turning to face the bodyguard pair, his hands gripped the phone tight enough to turn white.

"Fifteen years ago? Isn't that..."

Although he didn't finish the question, the pair seemed to understand what he was asking and nodded.

"Yes, Arturo Radcliffe was the primary suspect," Gavriil said. "He disappeared immediately after the shipment went missing. It's suspected that the fire was set deliberately to cover his tracks. He was hunted down, of course, but it took years to find him, and by then, it turned out he was already dead. Cancer got him before any of our people could. If he did steal the shipment, it was long gone by the time we found him, so it was never recovered."

The explanation made no sense, and I felt like I was missing some vital information, but one word stuck out to me like a bomb going off in the middle of a symphony.

"Fire? What are you talking about? What do you mean 'set deliberately'? Stop speaking like I'm not here and explain it to me."

No one spoke immediately. Eva and Gavriil looked to D'Angelo, who was scrolling through the information on the phone again. His expression grew darker and darker, until eventually, he closed his eyes and just hung his head. A few uncertain moments passed before he jerked back into a proper, upright posture with a new glint of determination in his blue eyes. Yet, when he sat before me on the floor, his voice was warmer than I'd ever heard it.

"Oliver. I'm going to summarize everything for you, and I need you to listen and not interrupt until I'm done. Can you do that?"

Still huddled pathetically on the floor, I sat up a little straighter, wiped the frustrated tears from my eyes, and nodded.

He smiled. "Good boy."

Despite everything, the sound of that midnight velvet voice praising me still made me shiver.

He explained the truth as clearly and simply as possible, but nothing could soothe the horror that swelled in me as I listened.

My father, Arturo Radcliffe, was a member of the Italian mafia. Specifically working for the Vidales family. Fifteen years ago, the Italian mafia and the Russian mafia had been in the middle of establishing a trade deal that used the Baltimore harbor, but it had fallen through when one of the shipments had been stolen.

My father was suspected of being the thief because he disappeared right after the theft happened. The fire that burned down my childhood home destroyed all traces and records of him, making him much more difficult to track down, which meant he had likely set the fire intentionally. That was how he'd gotten away with it.

Now, the Russian and Italian mafia were trying to reestablish the same trade deal that fell through fifteen years ago, but just like back then, another shipment had gone missing. It was why D'Angelo was here in Baltimore in the first place, to figure out how to solve the mess and stop the Italians and the Russians from declaring war on each other.

"Do you understand?" D'Angelo said after he'd finished summarizing everything.

Sometime during his explanation, unnoticed by me, he'd grabbed both my hands and held them tightly.

"Because of this, it's even more important than I realized that you stay here where I can protect you. If the Russians figure out that your father was probably the thief fifteen years ago, now that the situation seems to be repeating, you're going to be the number one suspect now. You wouldn't survive their interrogation. My own people I can handle. They won't touch you without my permission, but I don't have any control over the Russians. If they get their hands on you, I may not be able to save you in time."

I heard his words. They flowed between the crevices of my brain like water, delivering their meaning directly into my thoughts. Yet, I couldn't put in the effort to remember what he said.

Instead, I just squeezed his hands so hard that both of our fingers were going numb.

"They knew."

"Oliver?" D'Angelo started to say, but I cut him off.

"They fucking knew. My Mom and my Grandma. They must have known about my father, and they never told me."

My hands were shaking so bad I couldn't hold onto him anymore. I stood up and started pacing. In the back of my mind, I noticed D'Angelo signal Eva and Gavriil to leave, but I didn't stop to think about it.

"The fire. He set the fire intentionally. Did he know we were in there? Did Mom and Nana know? They said it was an accident."

Memories flashed in my mind.

The despair I'd felt when I first woke up in the hospital to find half my face covered in bandages. The nurses, my Mother, and my Grandmother all comforted me, telling me it was just an accident. That these things happen, and we need to rise above them. Every time I got upset about it after, they always responded the same way.

"It was just an accident. There's no reason to get so upset. These things just happen."

But it wasn't an accident, and they knew. Maybe they didn't know that Rowan and I were still in the house when the fire was started, but they must have realized afterward that my father had set it intentionally.

Yet they kept repeating those useless platitudes that did nothing except make me feel guilty for getting upset.

"Oliver."

D'Angelo's sharp voice broke me out of my memories. He yanked my hands away from my body, holding tight to my wrists, and I realized I'd been scratching at my left arm. It was the one with the burn scars on it. I used to scratch at the scars when I was younger, but I'd eventually been scolded out of the habit. Now, it seemed old habits were coming back.

"They stole my face." Tears were dripping down my cheeks, hot against my flushed skin. "They burned it right off me, and they did it intentionally. They didn't even have the decency to tell me."

"Hey, nothing was stolen." D'Angelo let go of my wrists to try and soothe me, wiping the tears off both my cheeks. "Your face is right here, and it's beautiful because it's you. I'm sure your father didn't know you were in the house when he set the fire, and the rest of your family didn't tell you because they didn't want you to worry."

What he said made sense, but I didn't want to hear it. I didn't want to hear anything.

It was just like the nights when I didn't want to work at the club, but I had to get out on stage anyway. Or the mornings when I was exhausted from working late, but I still had to get up for an early shift.

Shut my brain off. Focus on something else. Let my body go on autopilot.

There was no decision. One moment, I

was standing there staring up at D'Angelo as he dried the tears from my cheeks, and the next I'd grabbed him by the lapels of his jacket and pulled him down into a kiss.

It felt great. The press of lips against my own chased away all other thoughts, like leaves caught in a cool autumn wind. Soothing, yet also warm and stimulating. I could have stayed there for the rest of my life.

Yet, only a moment later, D'Angelo was pulling me away.

"Oliver, this isn't…"

"Yes, it is," I cut him off before he could finish, not wanting to hear him speaking logic right now. "It's fine. I want to. I just… I need to think about something else. Feel something else. Something other than numb, or angry. Please." I tried to reach for him again. "I need this."

"You don't…" He trailed off, looking around himself as if just now realizing we were in the front room of the penthouse. Eva and Gavriil had disappeared somewhere, but the open area still lacked privacy.

Grabbing my wrist he pulled me into

the master bedroom, then closed and locked the door.

Perfect. That was just where I wanted to be.

I twisted my fists in his shirt again and tried to pull him back to me, but he pushed me away before our lips even touched.

"Wait, Oliver. Stop. I just wanted to get us some privacy. You're upset. This... isn't a good idea."

Growling low under my breath, I lashed out and shoved at his chest. He must have been shocked because I actually managed to make him stumble backward.

"I'm so sick of being good. I've been *good* all my life. Don't be upset. Get a job as soon as you can. Get two jobs. Work under the table. Work nights. Help the family. Take care of your brother. Handle the bills. Don't complain. I'm so fucking sick of it!"

The strength suddenly left my legs and I collapsed onto the foot of the bed. "I'm so tired, but I didn't mind. I thought my family was just unlucky. We were all victims of fate, and we were all making sacrifices. How could I complain when my brother's health was worse than my scars, and my mother was just as tired as I was?"

My tears returned, and this time I started hiccupping. "It's not fair. I've been trying so hard to be *good*, and all this time they were lying to me. What's the point of being *good*? What does it get me? I haven't even told my family about half the things I do to make money because I thought they'd be ashamed. All so I could stay *good* in their eyes. But it's all pointless."

I'd started scratching at my scars again, this time focusing on the scar covering my face. My nails dug into the uneven skin until a sharp prick told me I was about to draw blood.

D'Angelo knelt in front of me and yanked my hands away from my face.

"Stop that. You're going to hurt yourself."

"So what?" I argued. He still held my wrists and I struggled to free myself, not sure if I wanted to hit him or pull him closer.

When that didn't work, I leaned forward until our foreheads touched. "Please. Please just give me something else to think about. I can still see it. The fire. I can still smell it. The smoke and heat are trapped in my skin. Please, just..."

When I looked at him, his image was blurry, and I realized I'd started crying again.

"Please just help me not think for a while."

This time, he didn't immediately push me away. He let go of one of my wrists to wipe my tears away, but the moment he did, my free hand started scratching at my scars again. This time focusing on the ones on my chest.

That seemed to decide it for him.

In one impressive move, he wrapped his arms around me and picked me all the way up. I was weightless for a moment, suspended only in his arms, then he deposited me at the head of the bed. I bounced on the mattress but was immediately pinned down by his weight as he straddled my hips.

With one hand, he kept control of my wrists, and with the other he started undoing his belt.

I squirmed in anticipation. Although I'd never actually gone this far with sex,

I'd been eager for it practically since the moment I met him, and now it seemed I was finally getting what I wanted.

All it took was a complete emotional breakdown.

However, once his belt was off, he kept the rest of his clothes on. Instead, he used the belt to lash both my wrists above my head to the bed's headboard.

"There," he sighed as he sat back to admire his work. "No more hurting yourself." I started to protest, but he pressed a finger against my lips to silence me. "Don't worry. I'm going to take care of you. But we're doing this my way. You're too self-destructive right now to make good judgments."

He climbed off the bed and I whined in the back of my throat. The belt bit into my wrists, which was some physical sensation at least, but it wasn't what I'd been hoping for.

D'Angelo didn't go far. He searched through the closet for a moment before coming back with a medium-sized, nondescript box, which he placed on the bedside table. Studying me for a moment, he then opened the box and pulled out several lengths of soft nylon rope.

"That belt's going to cut off your circulation. Here. This'll work better."

He untied my hands, but I wasn't free for long. Using the rope, he tied one of my hands to one bedpost, and my other hand to the opposite bed post so my arms were splayed in a 'Y' shape. He was right, the ropes were soft and a lot more comfortable than the belt had been. I was actually able to relax and enjoy the sensation.

Especially, when he climbed back over top of me and started kissing down my neck. My shirt was in the way, so he ripped the fabric right off me, exposing my upper body. He'd never seen the scars on my chest before, but I wasn't surprised when he barely seemed to notice them.

His kisses trailed over my skin, covering scars and smooth skin equally. I squirmed the lower he went, until he'd kissed a path all the way down my stomach to the top of my pants.

Dark blue eyes looked up at me. "Tell me to stop and I will. This is about making you feel good."

I desperately shook my head. My whole body was already trembling. "No. Keep going."

My pants were removed a lot easier than my shirt, and for the first time, I was completely bare in front of him. In fact, it was the first time I'd been completely naked in front of anyone since my burns first turned to scars. Half the time I couldn't even bear to look at myself in the mirror, yet D'Angelo didn't hesitate.

Grabbing both my legs, he kissed a path up one thigh from knee all the way to my hip, then repeated the process with the other leg.

Then getting comfortable on the bed, he took my already hard cock in hand and started kissing there as well. The light kisses sent sparks of pleasure dancing across my eyes, but it wasn't enough. He was just teasing me. I squirmed and tried to wrap my legs around him to pull me closer, but he braced one hand on my hip to hold me in place.

"Patience. Just relax and enjoy it."

Relax.

Right.

How was I supposed to relax when he started dragging his tongue up and down my shaft?

With my arms tied to the bedposts, I

couldn't even cover my face to hide my embarrassment. All I could do was lie there and let him do whatever he wanted with me.

"Please," I begged. "Please, more."

He stopped, and I cried out from the sudden loss of sensation.

"Don't worry." His voice was low and soothing, like he was talking to a spooked animal. "I'm not leaving you alone. I just need to get something."

From the box by the bed, he pulled out a bottle of lube. Coating two of his fingers in the clear gel, he returned to his previous position and opened my legs a little wider.

"Just relax and stay soft for me. I promise this'll feel good."

His fingers probed between my legs, starting at the base of my cock and sliding downward until they slipped inside the cleft of my ass. I whined and nearly bit my tongue as he smeared the lube around the rim of my hole. The cool liquid along with the feel of his skin provided an odd contrast of sensations.

"How much have you had inside you before?"

He had to repeat the question several

times before I heard him.

"Two... two fingers." I writhed, and my legs seemed to have a mind of their own as they tried to kick out. "I could never get a third one in."

"Well, then, this shouldn't be too hard. Deep breath."

I tried, I really did, but my lungs felt like a snake was constricting my chest and all I could do was pant as one of his fingers slid inside me. At the same time, his mouth descended on my cock, and he swallowed me whole.

I screamed.

The two sensations at once were too much. I felt electrocuted, but it didn't hurt. I unintentionally pulled at the ropes around my wrists as my whole body seemed to come alive at once.

His head bobbed between my legs, pulling off my cock then swallowing me again, over and over. At the same time, his finger thrust in and out of me, probing at my inner muscles until he hit a spot that made stars dance in my vision. Every muscle in my body locked up in pleasure so I couldn't even make a sound.

I lost track of time. My whole body felt like one big nerve ending, and I barely noticed when a second finger slipped inside me. The extra stretch just added a new sensation to the already overwhelming chaos.

He kept it up, thrusting his fingers into me harder and deeper while he continued to lave attention on my weeping cock. The pleasure built up inside me, tighter and tighter, until all at once my entire nervous system seemed to explode.

Even once it was over, I took a while to come down. He stayed between my legs pressing little kisses over my hips and stomach as he waited for me to catch my breath.

When my brain no longer felt like it was running out of my ears and I could finally string two thoughts together, I looked over to the side of the bed with a curios expression.

"What else is in the box?"

CHAPTER NINETEEN

D'Angelo

"WHAT ELSE IS in the box?"

Oliver had recovered faster than I expected, especially considering his sexual inexperience, so I wasn't prepared for the question. I stared at the box, and for a moment even I couldn't remember what it contained.

The throbbing arousal still trapped in my pants and stealing all the blood from my brain probably didn't help.

After an awkward moment of silence where my brain struggled to reboot, I grinned at him.

"Just a few toys I thought would be

fun."

Rummaging through the box with one hand, I pulled out a couple of basic vibrators. There was more, but I figured Oliver wouldn't be ready for anything too intense, so they stayed in the box.

Maybe another day.

Oliver stared wide-eyed at the three different vibrators I laid out on the bed for his perusal.

"Why do you have a box of sex toys?"

I shrugged, not at all self-conscious. "I thought they would be fun."

Shaking his head, Oliver still couldn't look away from the objects on the bed. "Yeah, but... you said you were only staying in Baltimore temporarily." He finally looked away from the vibrators to narrow his eyes at me. "Did you buy those specifically with the hope of using them on me?"

Picking up one of the toys—a moderately sized green dildo that vibrated and had rotating ball bearings just under the silicone surface—and spun it between my fingers. "Just wishful thinking. I always like to plan ahead."

Hazel eyes watched the toy in my hand with uncertainty. "I'm not sure if that's hot, or creepy."

"Let's go with hot." I let the tip of the dildo trail over Oliver's thigh, turning it on for just a moment so he could feel the vibrations. "I thought green would be your color, but now I'm not so sure. What'd you think?"

When Oliver didn't immediately answer me, I set the toy aside and lay next to him, so we were more eye to eye.

"We don't have to use these if you don't want, but I have a feeling..." I tugged at the ropes still securing his wrists to the headboard. "You like things a little less... vanilla. But it's your choice. What do you want?"

He leaned as close as the restraints on his wrists would allow. It wasn't enough for us to kiss, which seemed to be what he wanted, but our foreheads did touch. "Why bother with toys when you could just fuck me for real?"

He spread his legs open further in invitation.

I laughed. "Tempting, but not like this." I ran my hand down his torso until I grabbed one deliciously soft thigh. "When I do claim you, I'm going to do it properly. Right now, this is just about making you feel good to distract you from those overactive thoughts of yours. Not very romantic for your first time."

Oliver moaned low as I squeezed the sensitive flesh of his thigh a little tighter. Although he'd just come a few minutes ago, his cock twitched with excitement.

"The gray one," he finally said, his voice gruff and breathless.

I looked back at the toys waiting on the bed and frowned. "The gray one? But that's such a boring color."

"You're the one who bought it," Oliver mumbled. "You asked me what I want, and that's what I chose. Also..." He bit his lip, hesitating as he looked up at me through lowered eyelashes. "You should undress."

"What?" I asked, although my widening grin gave me away. I'd heard what he said; I just wanted to make him say it louder.

His eyes scrunched closed and his cheeks turned crimson, but he spoke with a full voice, practically shouting. "It's not fair that I'm the only one naked. You still have all your clothes. Take them off."

Standing from the bed, I gave him an over exaggerated bow. "How can I say no to such a command?"

Removing my clothes with care, I draped each piece over the nearby chair. I could feel Oliver's gaze on me the whole time. While I knew there was nothing for me to be ashamed about physically, I did wonder what he thought about the sight of my body. The cigarette burns on my chest and the old knife wound on my forearm that I'd shown him weren't my only scars.

Several bullet wounds decorated my body like starbursts, and slashing marks came in all sizes on my skin. There were even several claw marks over my shoulder blade from an incident where I'd tussled with a pack of attack dogs.

Overall, my body bore the evidence of the danger of my life. The scars were a reminder of who I really was, and I feared the sight of them would turn Oliver away.

However, he didn't even seem to notice, or if he did, he didn't care. He was too busy looking me up and down with hungry eyes.

I climbed back onto the bed and knelt over him. Despite my earlier statement, it was really tempting to just sink into him. If he weren't a virgin, I probably would have. I was certain that he would open so beautifully for me, but no one deserved to have their first time during a moment of such heightened emotion.

That was how I'd lost my own virginity. It was right after I'd taken someone's life for the first time, and the emotional backlash had convinced me to drag the first available person to bed.

Oliver deserved better than that, so I would control my own desires and content myself with bringing him pleasure in other ways.

Settling back between his legs, I propped a pillow under his hips for more support. With one hand, I selected the gray toy Oliver had picked out, and with the other, I grabbed the bottle of lube again. Although the toy was a boring color, I understood why he had picked that one.

It was the same reason I'd bought it in the first place. It not only vibrated, but also moved, shifting back and forth to provide as much stimulation as possible. Along with the subtle ridges sculpted along the shaft, it should easily drive him wild.

After slicking the vibrator with lube, I

kissed him just because I could. I felt him trembling, but the heated look in his eyes, and the way he eagerly tried to wrap his legs around me, said it was from anticipation rather than fear.

Pressing a few quick kisses to his neck, I moved down his body and slipped a pair of fingers inside him. He was still open from my earlier ministrations, so it didn't take long until I felt confident that he would easily be able to accept the toy.

Lining up the head of the vibrator with his hole, I nipped at his thigh, which rested near my head. "Deep breath and relax for me."

He nodded but didn't say anything as he let his head rest against the headboard.

As I'd hoped, the toy slipped inside him without too much resistance. The sound of his moan sent my already burning arousal into overdrive. His legs twitched and writhed as the toy settled deeply inside him, and his breathing turned erratic.

I gave him a moment to adjust, before turning on the toy to the lowest setting.

The response was instantaneous. Oliver keened as his senses were overwhelmed, and his whole body writhed like an eel. If not for the ropes tying down his wrists, he would have probably squirmed right off the bed.

Turning the vibrator up to the next level, I started shifting it around inside him, looking for his sweet spot, which I'd found earlier.

I knew I'd hit the right spot when his whimpers turned to actual begging.

"Mmmm. Please. Oh, fuck. Please. I... Ah, so good."

I could have listened to his pleading all day. Toying with him was a heady feeling. He was helpless under my hand, and his pleasure was mine to control.

Giving in to my sadistic urges, I turned the vibrator up two more levels at once, and kissed him to swallow his shocked cries. He was trembling so hard; I knew he was close to his end.

So was I. The taste of Oliver's desperation was too intoxicating for me to withstand for long.

Using my free hand, I started stroking my own cock in the same rhythm that I moved the vibrator inside him. If I closed my eyes, I could almost imagine I was fucking him properly, especially when I made cute little noises with each thrust of the toy.

We finished at the same time, gasping into each other's mouths as we both spilled over his stomach.

With my face buried against his neck, I slowly regained my senses. Once I could breathe normally again, I untied his wrists, and pulled him into my arms so he lay with his head pillowed on my chest.

His hand stroked the scars lying directly over my heart. "The toy was fun, but you said you wanted to claim me properly."

I idly untangled a few knots in his hair. "Yeah. This was just an emotional release for you. When I'm finally inside you for the first time, it should be more special than this."

He nodded, practically burying his face against my chest so that his words tickled my skin. "That means you... want to keep seeing me?"

Tipping his head up to face me, I looked directly into his eyes to give his words the consideration they deserved. "Why wouldn't I? If anything, I'm surprised you still want to see me."

It was only when I said it out loud that

I realized he never actually claimed he wanted to continue seeing me. The thought that this might be our only time together had crossed my mind, but it didn't feel real until that moment.

He didn't hold my gaze for long and soon looked down with a hint of sadness staining his expression. "I just thought, if my father was a part of your organization, and he stole something from you fifteen years ago that got you in trouble with the Russian mafia—God! That is so weird to say—then it would make sense if you don't trust me anymore."

Grabbing his hand, I pressed a kiss to his palm. "I still haven't pieced everything together, but I know one thing for certain. Your father's actions have nothing to do with you. He was a selfish man who stole what wasn't his and ended up hurting you in order to save himself."

"Yeah." Oliver spoke the word like a sigh as his hand started running over my chest again.

At first, I thought he was just seeking comfort, but then I realized he was counting the cigarette burn scars on my chest.

When he counted the last one, he

finally looked up and met my eye again. "You said your father did this to you?"

Removing his hand from my chest, I laced our fingers together instead. "Don't misunderstand. These weren't done out of hatred or a desire to hurt me. In fact, they're an expression of love."

Oliver raised a skeptical brow and looked at me like I was crazy.

I laughed and kissed his forehead.

"It's true. These were to help me learn how to handle pain. I was destined to take over as head of my family one day, and someone in my position would inevitably face a lot of danger. The ability to endure pain has saved my life more than once. These scars are a symbol that my father loved me enough to ensure I would survive no matter what."

Although he still didn't seem to fully believe me, Oliver nodded and let his head rest back on my chest. "I'll have to take your word for it. I guess family is just always complicated." He paused for a moment, and I felt him relax as his exhaustion caught up with him. "My family. I need to speak with them. I need to hear, from their own mouths, why they never told me about my father's mafia connection and that the fire might have been intentional.”

“Of course.” I planted one last kiss on the top of his head as he fell asleep. “I want to speak with them as well. They might have some of the answers that I need.”

I waited for a while, watching Oliver sleep. At least recent events hadn’t affected his rest, for he seemed perfectly at peace. Eventually, when I was certain he was deep in his dreams, I slipped out of his arms and headed for the bathroom. I took a moment to clean myself up, then returned with a warm washcloth to do the same for him.

With each gentle stroke of the washcloth, I worshiped every inch of his skin. Both the smooth and the scarred. The damage to his chest hadn’t been as bad as on his arm, or his face. In fact, his face seemed to have been hurt the worst. This struck me as odd at first. Usually, when someone was hurt, their first instinct was to protect their face. The arm probably should have been the worst, as it would have been used as a shield for the rest of him.

Almost as soon as the question popped

into my mind, the answer immediately followed. Oliver had used his arm as a shield, but not for himself. His arms had been occupied with protecting his brother, leaving his face completely exposed. Since skin on the face was more delicate than the rest of the body, it hadn't stood a chance without protection.

The image of a younger version of Oliver stumbling his way unprotected through a raging fire brought an unexpected wave of emotion surging up in my chest. I wasn't usually the type to get so interested in other people's struggles, but something about this man had cut right to the heart of me from the very first moment I met him.

Cupping his face, I pressed a quick kiss to the scarred skin of his check, then tucked the sheet around him and left him to sleep.

Then I stood from the bed and threw my clothes back on. They were wrinkled, and my hair was a mess. There was no hiding what I'd just done, but it didn't matter.

Eva and Gavriil had certainly seen me in worse condition.

Stepping out of the bedroom and

closing the door behind me, I found my bodyguards waiting in the penthouse's office.

We regarded each other silently for a moment until Eva lowered her eyes to the floor. "I won't apologize. It's my job to take care of any threat to you, and I'm not yet convinced that boy isn't a threat."

For the moment, I ignored Eva's use of the word 'boy' to describe Oliver. While he was younger, and much more inexperienced, he was far from being a child. Especially not after what we'd just done. However, there were bigger concerns to worry about.

Brushing some of the wrinkles from my clothes, I gave both of my bodyguards a hard look. "He's not a threat to me. However, this is unusual for you. In the past when you suspected one of my lovers to be a traitor, you brought it to my attention and let me handle it. Why take it into your own hands this time?"

Eva and Gavriil shared a glance, looking unusually bashful.

This time it was Gavriil who spoke up, stepping forward just enough to ensure he had my attention. "Well, Boss, you seem more... invested this time. You've never put so much effort into dating someone before."

"And you think I lack... conviction."

My clothes were as fixed as they could be. With one last tug at the cuffs of my shirt, I stepped closer until I was almost in the pair's personal space. Without warning, I grabbed each of them by the lapel. "I will say this once. Any threat will be eliminated without hesitation. *Any* threat."

Silently, both Eva and Gavriil nodded. Although I was indirectly threatening them as well, they actually seemed comforted by my little display.

Like a pack of wolves, they needed to be reminded that their Alpha still had the power to lead them.

Smoothing their clothes back into place, I patted them both on the shoulders and then took a seat behind the office desk.

"Now, tell me everything you've learned about Oliver's family. I know you two wouldn't have just left it alone after finding out about Arturo Radcliffe. He supposedly died a few years after stealing from us, right? Is that really the truth?"

Eva and Gavriil sat in the chairs on

the other side of the desk, spines as straight as iron rods.

"It seems to be true," Gavriil said. "We've found the coroner's report. Arturo Radcliffe really did die of cancer."

"Karmic," Eva added with a wry twist to her mouth.

Gavriil paused for a moment to see if she had anything else to add, then continued with a bit more exasperation in his voice. "However, we did come across something odd. The reason we didn't immediately make the connection between Oliver and Arturo Radcliffe was because the whole family switched to using the mother's maiden name. Including Oliver's Grandmother, who is actually his father's mother."

Pulling out the knife stored on the desk, disguised as a letter opener, I idly twirled the blade between my fingers.

"That is odd. Changing her name would make sense if she doesn't want to be connected to someone who stole from the Italian mafia, but why change to her daughter-in-law's maiden name instead of her own?"

Eva slid an actual paper file across the desk toward me, which held even more info than what I'd seen on Gavriil's phone earlier. "We looked into that, too. Oliver's Grandmother currently goes by the name Ingrid Grant, using her daughter-in-law's last name. Her married name was Ingrid Radcliffe. But her maiden name was Ingrid Falke. When we looked into the name Ingrid Falke, we got an odd response."

Looking through the information, I watched Eva and Gavriil over the top of the file. "Odd, how?"

The pair shared another look that had the hair on the back of my neck standing on end.

"Well..." Gavriil hesitated, which wasn't natural for him. "When we asked our contacts about the name Ingrid Falke, they were unusually keen to avoid talking about her. A bit too... insistent that they knew nothing."

"Your contacts?" I repeated. "You mean your Russian contacts."

Although they were loyal to me, Eva and Gavriil had originally been a gift from my Russian relatives as a sign of good faith between our organizations. That meant they had Russian connections that even I couldn't contact. It often came in handy, and in this case, it added to my suspicions.

"What do the Russians have to do with Oliver's Grandmother? I don't like having so many questions without answers. How was Oliver's father, a low-level enforcer, able to get away with stealing so much from us without getting caught? How are the Russians connected? Why has information been so hard to get a hold of?"

I slammed the knife into the desk, the blade sinking nearly two inches into the wood.

"Something isn't adding up."

CHAPTER TWENTY

D'Angelo

THE NEXT DAY, just as I promised, I took Oliver to meet with his family.

We stopped at his friend's place first to check on them. After what happened to him at the coffee shop, Oliver was concerned for Ashes's safety, but he also knew that once he started questioning his family, he would probably be there for a while and wouldn't have time to look in on his friend afterward. So, making a quick stop at Ashes's place first was the simplest option.

"Your friend lives in a shack?" I asked as we sat in a car across the street from

Ashes's residence.

At first, I thought that the actual house on the property was our destination, until Oliver told me that the house belonged to Ashes's landlord. Apparently, Ashes lived in the outbuilding in the back. It couldn't hold more than a room or two, and looked like the kind of place where lawn equipment would be stored.

"Ashes uses it as a workshop for their jewelry business," Oliver explained. "There's a bed and a kitchenette in there as well, along with a small bathroom. It's basically like a studio apartment. They could probably afford more, but the workshop is the only thing they really care about."

I shrugged. "To each their own, I suppose." I still didn't understand why someone would choose to live like that, but I wasn't about to question Oliver's friend in front of him.

"Boss," Eva called to me from the front seat of the car. "We've got a problem."

Sighing, I resisted the urge to start tugging out my hair. "What is it now?"

"The security we set around this place. I can't get a hold of them."

That did not bode well. I only employed the best security. They wouldn't be out of contact for anything other than an emergency situation.

There wasn't time to worry about it. We needed to act.

"All right. I'm going in. Eva, come with me. Gavriil, stay with Oliver."

"But, Boss—" both Eva and Gavriil started to argue.

"No. Do as I say. One of you stays with Oliver. Someone's already tried to kidnap him once before. All of this will be for nothing if he ends up getting taken anyway. If we're not seeing anything from out here, that means whatever happened is already over, or only a small group was sent after Ashes. Either way, we can handle it."

Oliver tugged desperately at my arm, nearly pulling my jacket off my shoulder. "Did something happen to Ashes? They're okay, right?"

Giving his hand a squeeze, I tried to sound as reassuring as possible. "I don't know. That's why I'm going to go in there to find out. You're going to stay here so Gavriil can keep you safe."

"What? No!" Oliver reached for the door

handle. "If something happened to Ashes then I'm going in with you."

I grabbed him by both arms and pulled him back before he could get the door open. "No. Oliver. You're going to stay here. If you go in, you'll only put yourself in danger and there's nothing you can do. Don't make me restrain you."

He was panicking and his pupils were contracted to mere pinpoints, but he swallowed his racing pulse and managed to nod.

"All right, fine. But you better not take too long."

I kissed his forehead. "Be back before you can blink."

After quickly checking that all of my weapons were in place, I jumped out of the car with Eva. We went around the edge of the property, sticking to the shadow of the decorative pine trees that lined the street. It was dusk, so the fading light worked to our advantage and blurred everything into an indistinguishable gray.

The shack—I refused to think of the tiny little building as a home—had two doors. One in front and one in back. It was an easy choice which one to take. The only windows were on the front wall, so there was no way to see someone approaching the back door from the inside.

I didn't even see any security cameras on the building. It really was an unsafe place.

The thought of Oliver spending a lot of time in this shack hanging out with his friend terrified me. When this was over, I was going to buy this Ashes person a new place to live just for my own peace of mind.

Without many windows, it was also difficult to check what was happening inside the shack before going inside. After quick deliberation, I decided an abrupt entry would be necessary. If we turned out to be wrong and there was no danger, I would simply apologize to Oliver's friend later, but I was nearly certain that wouldn't be the case.

Standing to either side of the back door along with Eva, I quietly counted to three. Then, using all my strength, I kicked in the door. The wood practically splintered under my foot, but it opened and allowed Eva to charge inside.

Gunshots rang out before I could even follow her through the door. Shouldering my way inside, I found the shack to be exactly as Oliver had described. One corner almost looked like an apartment, with a bed, couch, television, and a kitchenette. However, most of the space was dedicated to a jewelry-making workshop. Everything had a chaotic sort of order to it.

Except for one table, which was just chaos without the order. It had been overturned, and various tools and materials lay scattered over the floor.

My brain had about five seconds to catalog everything I was seeing. Several people stood over a bound figure on the floor.

Based on Oliver's description, the figure was Ashes. They were squirming against their bonds and trying to look around in a panic, but the blindfold over their eyes made everything they did useless. I didn't recognize their attackers, but I knew a kidnapping when I saw one.

Eva had already engaged the first kidnapper by the time I reached the group. Her bullets had killed at least one person, and another body lay conscious but bleeding on the ground. I managed to get a shot off, putting a bullet in the shoulder of the nearest kidnapper. They stumbled, but it wasn't a lethal shot.

The kidnappers naturally split down the middle, half focusing on me while the other half confronted Eva. Just from the way they moved I could tell they were seasoned fighters. Probably ex-military who fell on hard times after returning to civilian life.

This wouldn't be an easy fight. They were likely the same group of people who had attacked Oliver, and it seemed they'd learned their lesson and brought a larger group.

One of the kidnappers kicked a table at me, and I was forced to lower my gun in order to dodge out of the way. The shack was small. There wasn't a lot of room to maneuver. A gun was limited up close. If I tried firing again, I would just as likely shoot an ally as an enemy. Off to the side, Eva was also having a similar difficulty, but I had to trust her ability to handle herself while I concentrated on dealing with my half of the kidnappers.

Stowing my gun away, I pulled out a pair of long knives instead. I always liked bladed weapons better than guns, they felt more in control than a bullet that could fly off in any direction, and the hilts settled comfortably in my hands.

The next kidnapper I encountered swung at me with a nightstick. Flipping one of my knives so the blade lay along my forearm, I blocked the swing of the nightstick. The clang of metal against metal knocked the kidnapper off balance, and I pressed forward. I embedded my other knife in the kidnapper's neck, slicing right through a main artery.

With a spray of blood, the kidnapper dropped to the floor like the devil himself had snatched their soul right out of their body.

I did a quick count. There were at least three more kidnappers still alive from my half of the group.

My blades flashed. I swept out legs from under people, blocked blows when people tried to hit me, and dodged every time I saw the muzzle of a barrel point my way. Another kidnapper fell, and I couldn't even consciously remember what had killed him. My body moved on instinct and muscle memory. Very few actual decisions were required.

It was in these moments that I always felt the most free. No thought. No decisions. Just movement.

Something struck the back of my leg and my knee collapsed. Moving with the sudden change of momentum, I tucked into a roll and came up on the other side of the overturned table. This put me closer to Ashes's prone figure on the floor. At some point, they'd managed to get their blindfold off, and they stared at me with a mix of terror, confusion, and a little bit of recognition.

A shadow flickered in the corner of my vision. One of the kidnappers had tried to sneak up behind me. Reflexes kicked in, and I planted one of my knives in the middle of someone's chest. The blade struck their breastbone in an awkward way and twisted out of my hand. I knew better than to try and hold on and risk hurting myself. I let it go. The kidnapper collapsed, taking one of my weapons with them.

I could hear Ashes screaming behind the gag covering their mouth.

Rough hands grabbed me from behind and something sharp sliced my shoulder. I whirled around before they could get a proper hold on me and hugged their arm to my chest. Repositioning my feet for better balance, I threw my attacker over my shoulder. They flew through the air, feet tumbling over their head in a perfect arch, and hit the concrete floor with the satisfying crunch of breaking bone.

Unfortunately, my foot tangled in a coil of wire that had fallen to the floor and I tripped. My other knife fell from my hand, and for one terrifying moment, I was weaponless. My attacker saw the moment of vulnerability, and although they clutched their visibly broken arm, they still smiled in victory.

Adrenaline pumped through my veins, and I grabbed the first thing I could find. It turned out to be a soldering iron. The tool had a similar weight and handle to a knife, and I instinctively shoved the pointy end into my attacker's eye.

Only when I smelled something burning and heard the sizzle of flesh did I realize that the soldering iron was still on.

The kidnapper screamed and clawed at their eyes, desperate to get the iron out. I pushed deeper, all the way up to the hilt, until the flailing body stopped moving.

They finally collapsed and I stumbled back a step, breathing hard.

"What took you so long, Boss?" Eva

said from a few feet away.

Looking over at her, I found even more bodies lying on the floor at her feet. She'd dispatched her half of the enemies, and then dealt with a few of mine.

"What? You're the bodyguard. This kind of stuff is supposed to be your job."

She grinned at me—or at least gave me a toothy expression that passed for a grin—then stored her own knives safely back in their sheaths.

"You're slower than normal today. Did your new bedmate work you too hard?"

A muscle twinged in my lower back.

"Shut up."

I'd been so busy dealing with the Russians, and Caprice, and Oliver that I couldn't remember when I last got a decent night's sleep. Although, I would never admit such a thing. I'd much rather let Eva think that my fatigue was a result of overindulgence. I had a reputation to maintain, after all.

"Ashes!" Oliver's familiar voice shouted as he ran into the shack.

I cast a glance at Gavriil, who stood in the doorway.

The man merely shrugged. "What. You said keep him safe. You've taken out all the enemies. It's safe now."

I frowned at him but didn't argue.

Kneeling by his friend's side, Oliver pulled the gag from Ashes's mouth. "Are you okay? You're not hurt, are you?"

Ashes spit the gag out with such force they nearly bit their own tongue. "What the hell, Oliver? What's going on?"

"It's okay," Oliver tried to reassure them while removing the rest of the ropes. "You're safe now. Everything's being handled."

Ashes tried to immediately jump to their feet, but they were obviously dizzy and stumbled. Oliver caught them before they could fall.

"Okay?" Ashes continued to shout, though they let themself be guided to sit on the mostly untouched couch. "This is not okay. Oliver. Your boyfriend just killed a guy with my soldering iron. Everything is far from okay."

"There's an explanation. I swear. It's just that..." Oliver trailed off, looking pensive for a moment, before he turned to me. "Actually, why did they attack Ashes? My friend isn't connected to you."

I retrieved my knives from where they had fallen and checked the blades for damage. "No, but you are, and through you they could control me. Since their plan to kidnap you failed, they went after your friend to try and lure you out."

"Ah, I see..." Hazel eyes suddenly widened. "But, if that's true, then what about my family? They're in just as much danger as Ashes."

"Yes," I said, putting my knives back in their proper places. "Which is why we need to move quickly. Come on. Bring your friend. You can explain everything to them in the car."

CHAPTER TWENTY-ONE

Oliver

ASHES CAME WITH us, clinging to my hand so tightly that I was losing feeling in my fingers. They had accepted my explanation about D'Angelo and the Mafia surprisingly easily, though I wondered how much of that acceptance was simply shock.

The sun had fully set by the time the car pulled to a stop a few blocks from my house. Everything looked exactly the same as I remembered. None of the houses seemed disturbed, not even my own house, but that didn't guarantee anything.

Ashes's place had also looked fine from the outside.

Gavriil was sent out alone to scope out my house and see what was going on. As much as I wanted to just charge in and make sure my family was all right, the incident with Ashes demonstrated how dangerous that could be.

A few nerve-wracking minutes later, Gavriil returned to report that my family seemed fine and even the security that D'Angelo had assigned to guard them hadn't seen anything suspicious.

If it weren't for the close call with Ashes, as well as my own attack, I would think we were being paranoid.

"I'm going in on my own."

"Oliver, no," D'Angelo immediately argued.

I was already reaching for the door handle. "My family isn't in immediate danger right now. How do you think it'll look if you bust into the house, guns blazing?"

D'Angelo sniffed like he was offended, but his hand twitched toward the gun strapped to his hip. "I was planning on being more subtle than that."

"And what? You'll just show up and

start demanding answers about my father and my family? They don't know you. They have no reason to tell you anything."

From the front seat of the car, Eva's voice was even colder than usual. "We have plenty of ways to convince people to talk."

"And I'd prefer that you don't threaten my family." I had no idea where the confidence to challenge someone that had previously tried to kill me came from. It was like, from the moment I'd been thrown into this strange world of murder and Mafia, some part of my brain had just turned off. The rules of normal life had been thrown out. We were playing a whole new game now, and I was free to do or say anything I wanted.

D'Angelo placed a gentle hand over mine, which still rested on the door handle. "Just because it doesn't look dangerous doesn't mean it's actually safe."

I gripped the handle harder. "I know, but I still need to talk with them. Not only do I want answers, but if they are in danger then I need to convince them to come with us for safety."

We hadn't actually discussed what to

do with my family, but since Ashes had been allowed to come with us, I saw no reason why the same couldn't be true for the rest of the people I cared about.

D'Angelo nodded slowly then oddly started adjusting the collar of my shirt. "I figured you'd say that. All right. You can go in alone, but you're wearing this camera so we can see and hear everything that happens. If you're threatened, then we'll come get you. Meanwhile, we'll guard the house."

He added something to one of the buttons on my shirt. Like a little glass cap, it simply looked like a different style of button, but D'Angelo showed me the screen of his phone to reveal a live recording from my perspective.

"It'll be fine," I assured him, flashing him a smile I didn't truly feel. "I'm just going to talk with them. What could go wrong?"

Famous last words, but I refused to let my nerves show.

Sucking in a deep breath, I exited the car and headed toward the house. Stepping through the front door with the night sky hanging over my head made it feel like just another day of coming home after a late closing shift at the coffee shop.

Rowan was the first to notice my presence, sitting up in his chair and immediately forgetting the movie he was watching. "Oliver. You're back already."

Back already?

I was confused for a moment, until I remembered the cover story D'Angelo had made up about taking me away on a vacation.

My mother stood from the couch, wringing her hands as she looked between me and the kitchen. "We weren't expecting you back so soon. Have you eaten? I can make you something."

Rolling close enough to almost run over my foot, Rowan grinned mischievously up at me. "I'm sure his boyfriend didn't let him go hungry."

I ruffled his hair in the way I knew he hated. "Shut up, brat. You don't even know what you're talking about."

Scowling, he frantically tried to fix his hair. "Hey. I'm fifteen. Not five. I know about... that kind of stuff."

"You can't even say the word 'sex'. You definitely don't know what you're talking about," I teased, letting a grin touch my lips.

It was so easy to fall back into familiar banter with my brother and cast aside threats of Mafia and assassins.

But I couldn't ignore it. That wouldn't do anything except get us all killed.

"Actually, Mom. I do want to talk to you. Can we speak in the kitchen?"

The nervous movements of her hands increased. "Of course. What do you... I mean, yes. Let's speak in the kitchen."

It was no surprise when my grandmother joined us as well. She always insisted on being part of any gossip, and based on my tone they probably realized the weight of what I wanted to talk about.

Once all three of us were sitting around the kitchen table, with Rowan distracted by his latest monster movie in the living room, it was surprisingly my mother who spoke up first.

"I know what you're going to say."

"You... do?"

"Yes. I'm so sorry. It's all my fault. I don't know why I didn't notice sooner."

Now I was really confused.

Had she truly not known that my Father was a member of the Italian Mafia when they were married?

Or was she talking about the fire?

Her hands practically twisted themselves into nervous knots as they rested on the kitchen table. "I know about the money."

Huh?

My baffled expression must have been obvious, but my mother didn't notice.

She was too busy stumbling over her own words.

"Since you were going to be gone for a bit, I finally took a look at our finances for myself. I don't know why I let you talk me into taking care of the bills on your own." She finally met my eyes, and there were unshed tears clinging to her eyelashes. "We have a lot of debt, but it's significantly lower than it should be. Oliver..."

A few tears slipped from her eyes, and her chin wobbled as she struggled not to cry. "Oh, Oliver. I can't imagine what you've been doing to make that much extra money, but it's not... it's not... Please tell me you didn't do anything dangerous, or... or..."

She couldn't even bring herself to finish the statement as she broke down into actual sobs.

My extra night job at the club?

That's what she was so worked up over?

I knew what she was insinuating I'd done, and a month ago I would have been upset over the accusation. However, such concerns seemed inconsequential after everything else I'd recently experienced.

"Um, yeah." I scratched at my scarred arm, not sure what to say now that my expectations for the conversation had been derailed. "I have a night job. It's no big deal. I just didn't tell you about it because I didn't want you to worry that I was overworking myself."

"Did you sell yourself?" My grandmother's voice was surprisingly flat when she said this.

I jerked back so hard in surprise that my chair scraped against the floor. "What? No. I was hired to dance at a club. That's it."

My grandmother's expression didn't change. "I know what kind of club you're talking about. Even if no one touched you, you still sold your body for others' enjoyment."

"Nana..." My mother's hand slammed against the table. "That isn't helping.

Look, Oliver. We're not judging you, but that kind of... work... isn't safe. You need to stop. I know you're worried about our finances and taking care of Rowan, but it isn't your responsibility. This is for me to handle, and I've been pushing things off on you too much. You need to focus on living your own life."

Living my life?

That was going to be a lot harder while being targeted by the Mafia. Despite stepping into the house with a goal in mind, I'd let the conversation slip away from me, and I needed to get back to the real issue.

Placing my open hands on the table, I forced myself to stay calm.

"Rowan is my brother, so his health is my concern as well. However, that's not actually what I wanted to talk to you about."

Looking both my mother and grandmother in the eye, I channeled all the confidence I had.

"I know about my father, and about the fire. Why did you never tell me my father was a part of the Mafia, and that he set the fire intentionally?" I automatically raised my hand to touch my cheek, tracing the raised texture of the scars there.

In an oddly similar gesture, my mother also raised her hand, but she covered her mouth to control a new wave of sobs.

Silence wrapped the room in a stifling embrace. I would have wondered if I'd gone deaf, but after a minute my grandmother stood to start preparing a pot of tea, and the clink of porcelain seemed to ring as loud as church bells in the silence.

Eventually, she returned and placed a cup of tea in front of each of us at the table. Only after taking a sip did my mother finally collect herself enough to respond.

"Where did you learn about that?"

I swirled the teacup in my hands, watching the sugar dissolve in the drink. Tea wasn't as common of a selection at the coffee shop, so I didn't know as much about it. I didn't recognize the type, but it must have been a particularly strong flavor because the color was unusually dark. I couldn't even see the bottom of the cup.

Tea was supposed to be calming. I suppose my mother needed as much calm as could be condensed into a single cup.

"So, it is true. Dad really was a part of the Mafia, and he stole from them, then set our house on fire in order to help himself run away."

She didn't even try to deny it.

Gripping the cup in a tight fist, I angrily threw back half the drink in one go. It definitely had a strong taste, but I was too upset to even notice anything other than the heat on my tongue.

My mother cast a look toward Nana, as if waiting to see if the other woman had anything to add but was met with only more silence. Taking another sip of her own tea, she finally gave me an actual answer.

"Your father may not have been a good man, but he didn't intend to hurt you. You were supposed to be sleeping over at a friend's house that night, and he probably didn't realize that you'd come back early."

If she expected that to calm me down, it failed. In fact, it only made me angrier. I clenched my hand so hard around the cup that the porcelain cracked.

"I could believe that, but what about Rowan? He was only a baby. There's no way Dad didn't realize he was in the house."

My mother startled so badly she spilled her tea over the table. Brown liquid slowly seeped into the tablecloth, creating a stain that looked vaguely like a heart.

Nana stood and grabbed a wet towel from the sink to start cleaning up the stain. "It was probably meant to be one last gift for the family."

I watched her hands rubbing back and forth at the stain, and my stomach seemed to roll with the same rhythm.

"What do you mean gift? How could anything about this be considered a gift?"

The stain was better, but still present when Nana returned to the sink and rinsed out the rag.

"My son didn't always make good choices, but he did care about his family in his own way. Rowan's condition is expensive. He probably wanted to make sure we wouldn't be burdened with that expense after he was gone."

It took me a moment to realize what she was saying, but when I did, fury boiled my blood in my veins. My own father had intentionally tried to kill my brother, all in order to "save" us from having to deal with his condition. The coward stole from the Mafia and ran away for his own selfish reasons, then decided he could kill two birds with one house fire, securing his escape and getting rid of my brother at the same time.

"What the hell?"

The words echoed what I was thinking, but I wasn't the one who said them.

Off to the side, the door to the kitchen swung open to reveal Rowan, who must have been eavesdropping from the other room.

"Dad didn't... he didn't really... he couldn't have..."

Although he was a teenager, the tears that welled up in his eyes at that moment made him look like the same helpless child I'd carried out of the fire.

I jumped up from my chair to comfort him, but the moment my feet hit the floor the whole room spun. Desperately clutching at the table to try and stay upright, I looked over to see my mother slumped in her seat. The heart shaped stain, still only half cleaned, lay under her unconscious cheek.

Weakness hit me like a wave, making my whole body go numb. I collapsed, but just before I hit the ground, oddly, soft hands grabbed me and guided me down gently. My vision had already failed, and everything blurred together, so I couldn't see who held me, but I felt someone tugging at the button on my shirt with the hidden camera.

I tried to protest, but I didn't manage anything more than a useless croaking sound before my voice failed as well.

Then, like sinking into the depths of the ocean, everything faded to black.

CHAPTER TWENTY-TWO

Oliver

THE FLOOR WAS moving.

When I opened my eyes, everything around me seemed to be shifting back and forth. I felt dizzy, and nauseous, and my head was pounding so badly that I was surprised it wasn't leaking out of my eyes.

I was also sitting up. It was a strange position to wake up in, and I blinked dumbly at the sight of my own hands for several moments before I realized what I was seeing. I was tied to a chair, with my wrists bound to the armrests and my ankles bound to the metal legs.

The light around me kept shifting. My head lolled on my neck, so I was staring at the floor, and I watched as my own shadow stretched and shrunk. At first, I thought it was due to the dizziness I felt, maybe I was hallucinating, until I mustered up enough strength to look up.

A light hung from the ceiling above me, and it was swaying back and forth.

I felt even more nauseous just looking at it.

"Finally awake."

The unexpected voice startled me, but I didn't have enough energy to flinch. A woman I'd never met before stepped into my view. She had a barely noticeable Russian accent, and in some ways reminded me of Eva, but even more intense.

I didn't bother to respond. Her words hadn't actually been a question, so she wasn't looking for an answer. Plus, my mouth was so dry, I doubted I could speak anyway.

Grabbing the back of the chair I was tied to, she spun me around to face the rest of the room.

I first saw the sky outside a window that took up most of the far wall. Dawn was just starting to light the sky, adding pink highlights among the gray and black. I prayed it was the next morning and that I'd only been unconscious for a few hours, and not actually days later.

The next thing I noticed was the room itself. Suddenly, the swaying light made sense. It wasn't really a room at all. Rather it was the control booth of a large cargo ship. A long line of complicated control panels lay just under the window, and the front end of the ship stretched out beyond the glass, pointing toward the far horizon. Beyond the ship lay nothing but open sea.

All of these observations were noted and then immediately forgotten when my attention shifted again to the people in the control room with me.

The Russian woman was there, along with several other very intimidating people, but sitting calmly at a table in the center of the room was my grandmother.

"Nana? What?" The words scratched at my dry throat, but I had to speak up.

What was my grandmother doing here?

Had she been kidnapped, too?

She glanced at me, but her expression was like ice. If it weren't for the fact that I recognized her face, she would have seemed like a stranger.

It was too confusing to look at her, so I shifted focus back to the Russian woman instead. She was speaking to some of the other people in the room, saying something about 'International Waters'. I couldn't follow the full conversation, but it seemed important.

The man she spoke with also kept calling her Aslanov. I couldn't tell if it was meant as a first name, a last name, or a title, but it definitely sounded Russian.

These people were definitely the Russian Mafia. All the effort D'Angelo had put into keeping me from getting kidnapped, and I'd ended up in the hands of his enemies anyway.

How had I gotten here?

The last thing I remembered was sitting in the kitchen of my own house, speaking with my family.

My thoughts were interrupted when someone shoved open the door to the control room and ran up to Aslanov.

"The Bianchi leader has shown up, just as you expected. He's demanding to be let onto the ship."

Aslanov faced the window that looked

out over the ship, hands clasped behind her back like she was standing at military attention.

"Are we far enough out?"

"Yes," someone else answered, pointing toward something on the control panels. "We've just crossed the maritime boundary and are now on the high seas."

She nodded. "Very good. Let him aboard, but only him. His bodyguards and anyone else he may have brought with him must stay behind."

People immediately started moving around the room, but Aslanov stood like an unmoving pillar among the chaos.

"Oh..." She glanced toward me. "Gag him. We don't want any disruptions."

She had barely finished speaking when someone outside of my view shoved a wad of cloth into my mouth. Another strip of cloth was wrapped around my head to hold it in place. The cloth strip was secured so tightly it cut into the sides of my mouth, and the gag clung to my already dry tongue.

Even if I shouted, I wouldn't have been able to make a sound.

After that, no one paid me any attention. Even my own grandmother, who continued to sit like an unmoving statue at the room's only table, completely ignored me. I'd never felt more invisible in my life. There were plenty of times when I'd wished I could disappear, especially when people were staring at my scars, but right now I wanted nothing more than for someone to talk to me. Even if they didn't explain what was going on, just a few words of assurance would have been enough.

Someone grabbed the back of my neck in one broad, cold hand, and the hard barrel of a gun pressed against my head. The twitch of a single finger would be enough to end my life.

Like dangling over an abyss by a spider's threat, I was afraid to move or even breathe too deeply for fear of that lifeline snapping.

Moments later, the door to the control room opened again, and this time D'Angelo's familiar figure stepped through. Until then, I'd never really seen him in full Mafia Boss form. Even when he was literally killing someone in front of my eyes, it didn't have the same effect as it did right now. He almost didn't look human. Everything about him was perfect. Not a hair hung out of place, and his all black suit was pressed so sharply that he could have sharpened his knives on the creases.

Even the expression on his face was cold and perfect. This was the kind of man who comfortably held life or death in his hands on a daily basis.

For the briefest moment, his blue eyes flickered in my direction, but he almost immediately looked away and focused on Aslanov.

Even D'Angelo was ignoring me. Maybe I really had become invisible. I sunk in my seat, but then the gun at my head dug harder into my scalp and I sat up straighter.

Aslanov regarded D'Angelo with a sarcastic curve to her lip. "What? No tearful reunion? You're a rather cold lover, aren't you."

In contrast to her almost teasing tone, D'Angelo's expression never shifted. "I never let pleasure get in the way of business. I've killed people for less."

"Oh?" She gestured to the person standing behind me. "Then you won't mind if I just dispose of him."

The gun pressing against my head

gave a click as it was cocked, and the metallic sound echoed right through my skull.

Still, D'Angelo didn't even look at me.

He wasn't really going to let them kill me, right?

Up until now he'd fought to protect me. He wouldn't have done that if he could so easily throw me away.

Right?

It was at that moment I realized how short my relationship with D'Angelo had been. We'd only known each other a few weeks. That wasn't long enough to really get to know someone, let alone develop an actual commitment. Technically, what we had could still be considered a fling.

Someone so important and powerful wouldn't compromise himself for a mere fling. I was stupid to think otherwise. He protected me because it was the easier option, but now that I'd become an actual liability, he had no reason to protect me any longer.

Tears dripped from the corner of my eyes, soaking into the gag wrapped around my head. Forced to breathe only through my nose, I felt on the verge of hyperventilating as my lungs constricted from grief.

Still, D'Angelo continued to only pay attention to Aslanov, who was now fully smiling at him. After a moment of silence where nothing happened, he sighed deeply. "I'm not here for games. If that's all you're interested in, I'll deal with someone who actually knows how to get business done."

Then he turned away from Aslanov and sat at the table across from my grandmother.

"Ma'am." He gave her a slight nod.

My grandmother's face finally creased into an actual expression as she looked him up and down. "You don't seem surprised."

"Oh, I was," D'Angelo assured her with the hint of a smile on his lips. "But I think I've figured it out now. You've been here a long time, haven't you? Based on the timeline, it's probably been about forty years since you were put in place. That's a long time for a sleeper agent to stay dormant. I'm impressed."

Sleeper agent?

I'd only heard that term in old spy movies that Rowan sometimes watched when he wanted something other than monsters.

Did that mean... my grandmother was working for the Russian Mafia?

Or, no, it meant she'd been a part of the Russian Mafia from the start, and all this time had only been pretending to be an ordinary citizen.

The moment right before I passed out returned to my mind. I'd been in the kitchen, speaking with my family about my night job, and my dad's involvement with the Italian Mafia, and the fire. Then I'd suddenly passed out.

No.

Nana had served everyone tea, but now that I thought about it, although she poured three cups, I never saw her take a drink.

She'd drugged me, then handed me over to the Russian Mafia... because she was secretly a member of the Russian Mafia as well.

My head spun, and I swallowed several times to stop myself from throwing up. I had a bad feeling that if I threw up with the gag on, my captors still wouldn't let me take it off.

With her hands folded on the table, my grandmother was the very image of a polite lady. "It's your fault I was left dormant for so long. If you hadn't come along, I could have gone home a long time ago."

"Ah." D'Angelo nodded as if what she said made sense. "I wondered about that. You were put into position here when tensions between our organizations were high, but then my parents secured peace by getting married. So, you've maintained your persona as an ordinary citizen ever since, just waiting to finally be put to use." His grin turned sadistic. "Like an old toy waiting for its owner to finally play with it."

My grandmother sneered at him. "Enough. We all know the situation now, so there's no use repeating ourselves."

D'Angelo bowed his head ever so slightly. "My apologies. I just want to make sure everyone was on the same page."

For the briefest moment, while his head was bowed so no one could see his face, he glanced in my direction.

Realization struck like the first ray or dawn in my mind. Everyone else in the room knew the truth about my grandmother. There was no reason for him to say it out loud. He only did so to make sure I understood.

D'Angelo was talking to me. In this situation, he couldn't risk acknowledging me. That would only give his enemies more leverage against him. Yet, despite that, he still found a way to communicate with me.

My tears kept flowing down my cheeks, but now they were filled with hope instead of heartbreak.

CHAPTER TWENTY-THREE

D'Angelo

IT WAS HARD to tell since I couldn't look at Oliver for long, but it seemed like he understood my message. I wouldn't abandon him and would do my best to keep him in the loop about what was happening.

The watch on my wrist was new, so the sight of it on my wrist still seemed unnatural when I subtly looked down.

Not quite time yet.

Oliver's grandmother sat at the table across from me, her posture so perfect I could almost imagine the dangerous operative she once was.

What must it be like, to be trained into a lethal weapon, only to be put on the shelf and forgotten?

A sleeper agent who was never woken up. Surely that must have a negative effect on a person.

It seemed I wasn't the only one with these questions, for Aslanov stepped up next to the woman and placed a deliberate hand on the back of her chair.

"I have to say, madam, you are one of our most devoted agents. To live amongst the enemy for so many years."

She shook her head, a 'tisking' sound falling from her lips.

"Many agents have fallen for the trap of sentimentality before. Becoming too attached to their fake lives and failing to act when the moment finally arrived. When I first realized we had an agent here, I had my doubts, but this is one of the few times I'm glad to be mistaken."

Oliver's grandmother turned just enough to face Aslanov and tipped her head into a slight bow. "My duty has always been clear. If I am able to serve the Pahkan now, then my time will have been worth it."

"Glad to hear it. Glad to hear it."

Aslanov switched to the other side of the chair, her hand sliding along the back, so it just brushed against Oliver's grandmother.

Tension hung over all our heads like a guillotine blade. Despite her words, Aslanov's true intent couldn't have been more obvious. She didn't fully trust Oliver's grandmother.

That was fine by me. Let them waste time passive-aggressively arguing with each other.

Aslanov leaned closer so she was looming over the older woman's shoulder. "I'm curious, though. Were you relieved when the order to act finally came in? You could finally cast off your fake life and stop acting."

The ship under our feet rocked with the waves, so it was impossible to sit perfectly still, but Oliver's grandmother attempted it as she refused to face Aslanov directly.

"My feelings are not a factor, so there is no relief. Only actions matter, and my actions are always in service to the Pahkan."

"Hmmm." Aslanov rubbed her chin as if thinking, then sat directly on the table so she could loom even more efficiently.

I resisted the urge to roll my eyes. Such theatrics were... unnecessary. On an average civilian or even a lower-level subordinate, such posturing might be intimidating, but Oliver's grandmother was a seasoned spy. She'd likely received some of the best training the Russian Mafia had to offer. Aslanov's attempt to show dominance would have no effect.

Still, Aslanov pressed on with her performance. "In service of the Pahkan, hmm. Except, that's not really true, is it? Fifteen years ago, your son stole a shipment between the Italian and Russian families, and then disappeared. There's no way a low-level enforcer had the ability to pull off a heist like that on his own. You must have helped him. Now, I never agreed with that trade deal to begin with, so I approved of its disruption, but the fact stands that you took action without an order. One that disrupted the Pahkan's plans. Now, this can be forgiven since you weren't given any instructions, but I'm going to need some assurance that your loyalty is still intact."

While I still wasn't sure what Aslanov was angling for, I knew it couldn't be anything good. The two women were still distracted by each other, so I quickly glanced down at my watch again.

Just a few minutes left.

Finally, Oliver's grandmother moved more than a few muscles at a time. She stood from the chair with the grace of an aging queen and faced Aslanov directly. "Enough. State what you want plainly so that I may demonstrate my loyalty."

To my horror, Aslanov's gaze shifted toward Oliver.

I had been trying not to look at the other man, so that I could maintain my composure. The sight of him gagged and bound, which might have been scintillating in a more intimate setting, in this situation sent my blood boiling. The gun pointed at his head was enough for me to wish death on every single Russian on the ship.

Even myself, for getting Oliver into this situation in the first place.

Aslanov grinned like she had knives instead of teeth. "It's simple. Prove your fake life means nothing to you. Get rid of the boy, and then we can move onto more enjoyable matters."

She then, very promptly, handed a gun

to Oliver's grandmother.

I balled my hands into fists under the table. If they dared to harm a hair on his head, I would spill both of their guts over the floor.

Yet, the time wasn't right. I needed to stall.

Luckily, thanks to our previous meeting, I'd already figured out what annoyed Aslanov the most.

I laughed. "Aren't you forgetting something? We still have a trade deal to negotiate. That won't work very well if you get rid of your bargaining chip."

The response from Aslanov wasn't what I'd hoped. She merely smirked at me, like I was a child who'd just claimed that two plus two equaled five.

"Love must be clouding your brain, D'Angelo." I started to correct her, but she just held up her hand to silence me. "Don't bother. I've seen you swooning after this boy. You're quite besotted. I can't see why. He's certainly not going to win any beauty pageants, but I don't care about whatever weird horror fetish you have. All I care about is that you'll do whatever I want to keep him safe."

There wasn't really a point in denying

it. She'd already seen right through me. I probably should have been more discrete when pursuing Oliver, but I hadn't realized how dangerous the situation was for him until it was too late.

That was my failing, and if I wasn't careful, then Oliver would be the one paying for my mistake.

Since I didn't need to pretend any longer, I looked directly at him for the first time since setting foot on the ship. He looked terrified. The ropes on his wrists were chafing his skin raw and the gag was obviously biting into the corners of his mouth. I wanted nothing more than to rip them off him.

Breathing deep through my nose, I calmed my racing heartbeat.

"Fine. Even if what you say is true, then your little hidden spy here can't kill him. A dead hostage isn't very effective."

Aslanov laughed, and I seethed while she stood from the table with a dismissive wave of her hand. "He's already served his use as a hostage. He got you here, alone and unarmed." Pulling out a second gun, she pointed it right at me. "I don't need him anymore. The threat to your own life will keep you complacent. We're going to negotiate that trade deal, and you're going to sign over everything I want."

I wasn't sure who to focus on, the gun pointed at me, or the gun in Oliver's grandmother's hands that wasn't pointing anywhere yet.

This time I couldn't look at my watch without being noticed, but I could guess how much time had passed.

Soon.

"I may be the head of the Bianchi family, but perhaps you've forgotten that Alex Mariano is the true leader of our organization. It doesn't matter what I agree to if he doesn't agree as well."

Aslanov scoffed, and stepped closer so she was as close as possible while still out of my reach. "That spoiled Mafia Prince is too young to wield real power. Why else did he bring you in when he could have handled this situation on his own? He relies on you, and he'll do whatever you say he should do."

That wasn't a fair assessment of Alex, but it wasn't entirely wrong, either. If I wanted, I could probably convince him to go along with any negotiations I made, although it wouldn't be as easy as Aslanov made it seem. Alex was young and inexperienced, but he wasn't stupid. He'd been raised to be a leader, just as I was.

Crossing my arms and trying to act nonchalant, I tapped my foot against the leg of the table. "You're not the first person to threaten me, and death doesn't scare me. So, what happens if I don't roll over and give you whatever you want?"

It seemed nothing could upset Aslanov. Despite my blatant disregard for her threats, she merely shrugged.

"Then I kill you, and I go back to the Pahkan and say you attacked me first. He'll have no choice but to drop this trade deal entirely, which works for me. I don't like this deal to begin with. Either way, I get something I want."

Stuck within a dead-end argument, I grit my teeth and glared at her. No matter which option I chose, there was no winning.

When I didn't react, Aslanov seemed to grow bored and turned her attention back to Oliver's grandmother.

"We've wasted enough time. Kill the brat and let's get on with things. I've got better plans for you. I don't know why you were left to rot here, but it can work in our favor. An old woman with a sick grandson will gain a lot of sympathy. It's a great cover, and we can use it to our advantage. Who would ever suspect you? The possibilities are endless."

The mention of his brother stirred something in Oliver. He struggled against the ropes tying him to the chair and tried to shout through his gag. His grandmother watched him for a moment, but without a change in her expression, she lifted the gun in her hand to point directly at him.

Oliver froze, and my blood turned to ice. There was no way I would just let her shoot him. Even if it ruined our relationship with the Russians and caused a war between our organizations, he was getting out of here alive.

I was halfway out of my chair when a gunshot rang through the air. For one dreadful moment, I thought I'd acted too late. I waited for the horrible sight of Oliver's body slumping over within his bonds and the light fading from his eyes.

Yet, he remained alert. Terrified, but obviously alive.

Instead, his grandmother dropped dead to the floor.

"What?" Aslanov whirled around in the direction the gunshot had come from.

Alex Mariano's familiar form sat on the railing just beyond the window, holding an impressive looking assault rifle with the other. With one hand, he gave everyone within the room a cheeky wave, then cocked the gun again and took aim.

Time was up.

Not wasting a moment, I dove across the table and killed the pair of men standing on either side of Oliver with two quick slashes of my knife. They were dead before they hit the floor and forgotten even faster.

There wasn't time to fully untie Oliver. I cut just enough rope to remove him from the chair, then picked him up and started running. His weight bounced uncomfortably in my arms, and I could hear him shouting around the gag still in his mouth, but there wasn't time to explain. He was just going to have to trust me.

Well, even if he didn't trust me, he didn't have a choice anyway. He was coming with me whether he wanted to or not.

Slamming open the door that led from

the ship's control room out on the deck, I heard gunshots behind me but didn't stop to see who was firing. None of the bullets hit me or Oliver, so either it was friendly fire, or very badly aimed enemy fire. Either way, not my concern.

Still running, we reached the edge of the ship. There, I paused just long enough to remove the gag from Oliver's mouth.

"Take as deep a breath as you can," I told him, before jumping over the railing while still carrying him in my arms.

It was a long fall, and a harsh impact with the water below. To his credit, Oliver managed to not waste his air screaming, but I could feel him trembling in fear. Together, we hit the water and were immediately pulled under by the waves.

Despite the warm weather, the high seas were always cold. The temperature hit me like a punch to the gut, and I could only imagine what Oliver must be going through, still mostly tied up. Everything around us was dark, and as the current pulled us deeper, we quickly lost sight of the ship.

I pulled Oliver closer, and he curled against me. Then, with both of our lungs burning with the need to breathe, we waited.

Moments later, something grabbed my shoulder.

My initial instinct was to fight, but logic won over primal desires as a scuba mask was placed over my face. A second mask was then pressed into my hands, which I quickly slipped over Oliver's face as well. A pair of hoses connected to the masks supplied us with oxygen, and his trembling ceased once he was able to breathe again.

The mask also allowed me to see a little better under the water. It was still dark, but I could just make out a vaguely human shape, next to something long and sleek.

It was an underwater glider, with a small engine hidden inside its sleek body to propel it forward and handles along the outer shell for divers to hold onto.

The person currently floating next to the glider couldn't be identified in the dark, but I knew it was Eva.

Right on time, and all according to the plan.

Trying to cut off the rest of Oliver's ropes underwater would be more dangerous than it was worth. I merely held him close with one arm while grabbing onto the glider with the other. Eva also helped to steady us as the glider carried us through the water.

We didn't go very far before surfacing, maybe five hundred yards at most, but the glider wasn't particularly fast, so even such a short distance took a while to cover. When we finally surfaced, I was so relieved to feel fresh air against my skin. The ocean was a terrifying place, and I didn't like thinking about what could be lurking just out of sight in the depths below us.

A much smaller boat floated on the surface, where Gavriil waited for us. He helped get everyone on the boat, then dumped a bunch of towels on us before taking care of the glider.

I was finally able to get the rest of the ropes off Oliver, then started drying him off with the towels. He didn't say a word and let me position him however I wanted. Once he was done and as dry as he was going to get, he pressed against my chest and stayed there. I could feel him trembling, yet he didn't cry or even make a sound.

"What about the others?" I asked Eva

as I finished drying myself off.

"Mariano's people should be handling it. That bodyguard of his is surprisingly efficient for someone who was a civilian not too long ago."

I checked my watch, which was luckily waterproof. "Assuming everything is still on schedule, then we should be seeing the final conclusion right... about..."

An explosion rocked the heavens and turned the surface of the ocean into a chaotic tantrum. A fireball billowed up from the Russian's ship, illuminating the sky with orange light. The whole vessel seemed to have been practically cut in half, and immediately started sinking in a poor recreation of the Titanic.

Oliver whimpered and pressed closer to me. Although the Russian ship was at least five hundred yards away, warm firelight still illuminated the side of Oliver's face.

Knowing how he reacted to fire, I held him closer and cradled his head against my chest so he couldn't see the burning ship.

We watched the chaos in the distance for a moment as our little boat bobbed in the waves. After a few minutes, Gavriil finished with the glider and sat next to us.

"Do you think Aslanov survived?"

"Probably," I shrugged. "A sinking ship wouldn't kill that woman. Unless one of Alex's people got lucky with a bullet, we'll be seeing her again. However, a display of power like this from Alex will at least make the Russian's think twice about starting a war. They'll probably even respect him more now."

Gavriil grunted. "Pity. I was hoping Aslanov would go down with the ship. We could have used one less bitch in the world."

I raised an eyebrow at his unexpectedly crude language, but when I felt Oliver shivering against me, I couldn't help but agree. That woman had dragged Oliver through hell. She deserved to die.

Although, I'd also had a hand in what happened to him. I'd been the one to approach him in the first place, despite knowing how dangerous it was for anyone to associate with me. I wasn't blameless in this situation.

Maybe that meant I deserved to die, too.

In all the years of my life, it wasn't the

first time I'd asked myself that question. It was, however, the first time I didn't have a definite answer.

I was a killer with too much blood on my hands. Life had handed me an olive branch of innocence, and I couldn't help but feel like the universe was testing me.

What would I do?

If I was a decent person, I would let the olive branch go to avoid staining it with my sin.

Against me, Oliver shivered as a cool breeze blew past.

I held him tighter.

I never claimed to be a decent man.

CHAPTER TWENTY-FOUR

Oliver

IT HAD BEEN two weeks since the shootout on the ship, and I spent most of it sitting at home watching movies and playing video games with my brother. I hadn't returned to the coffee shop or Erodance. There was no telling how safe it was for anyone from my family to be out while things between the Italian and Russian Mafia were being settled.

Even my mother had spent the time home from work. Explaining everything to her had been odd. She'd been aware of my father's involvement in the Italian Mafia, but not that he had stolen from them, or

Nana's identity as a Russian sleeper agent.

Even just thinking about it two weeks later felt strange. Like the thought was too big to fit inside my brain and I could only examine pieces of it at a time.

After the two-week mark came and went, D'Angelo sent me a request to meet with him, shortly followed by a car to pick me up.

Gavriil was driving.

Maybe meeting with D'Angelo again after everything that happened was foolish, but I wanted closure. Even now that I had all the answers, things still didn't feel "finished". I'd been walking around in an almost trance-like state for the last two weeks, going through the motions of living without really feeling it.

Hopefully, speaking with D'Angelo would change that.

The penthouse was almost exactly the same as when I'd been there last, just emptier. Bare shelves no longer held a collection of books, there were no jackets hanging from the coat hooks, and overall, the place felt a little too tidy to be lived in.

"You're leaving," I said almost as soon as I stepped through the door.

D'Angelo looked up from his phone, sitting on the couch in the front room and obviously waiting for me.

"Yes. My time in Baltimore was only temporary to manage this deal with the Russians. Things are hashed out, mostly, so I need to move on to business elsewhere."

"Oh." I twisted my fingers around each other as I fought the urge to scratch at my scars. Not sure what to do with myself, I sat on the chair opposite him. Although only a few feet remained between us, it somehow felt very lonely sitting by myself when not that long ago I would have eagerly joined him on the couch.

I knew it was only temporary. I'd said it multiple times and never made any promises about the future.

So, why was I so blindsided to hear that he was leaving now?

"I guess it had to happen eventually."

I could adjust to this. I'd lived twenty-two years without D'Angelo. Learning to live without him again shouldn't be too hard.

My thoughts were turning over in my head so rapidly, I didn't notice when

D'Angelo stood from the couch and moved over to sit on the arm of my chair.

"Leaving is inevitable. I can never stay in one place for too long. However, I was thinking..."

He trailed off, and the uncertainty in his voice finally caught my attention. I looked up at him, and his hand cupped my scarred cheek.

"I was thinking... that you could... come with me."

His hand was warm on my skin, but I couldn't feel it. My entire body seemed to have gone numb.

"Come with you?"

"Yes." Grabbing my hands, he pulled me to my feet. "My position in the organization is dependent on my connections, so I'm always traveling around to meet with different people, but you could travel with me. Focus on your art instead of working, or just play tourist wherever we go. I don't care. I promise you won't be involved with things like you were this time. This was a... unique situation."

Unique was one way to put it. Finding out my father was part of the Italian Mafia was one thing. Finding out that my grandmother was also a secret Russian spy who'd been left dormant for decades, was a much more difficult idea to get my head around.

The fact that both of them had now nearly killed me at some point, nearly sent me into hysterics whenever I thought about it.

Had anything about my life up until now actually been real?

Well, there was one thing.

"But... my mother. My brother. I can't just leave them. Rowan needs someone to help take care of him, and his treatment is expensive. I can't let my mother support him all by herself."

"Oliver." He pulled me close. "I wouldn't expect you to just abandon your family. Nor am I asking this without offering anything in return. I can more than afford to support your family. Your mother wouldn't have to work at all, unless she wanted to. And your brother... I know you're used to supporting him on your own, but there are facilities that are specifically designed to handle his condition."

At first, the idea of sending my brother off to some care facility made me recoil and I pulled away from D'Angelo, so I stood alone in the center of the room.

My family had always taken care of Rowan on our own.

What could some random facility do that we couldn't?

Then an image of my brother dawned behind my eyes. Rowan sitting in front of the television, with only movie monsters for friends. His only interaction with other kids his age came through his online classes, and he celebrated the days he was able to get down the stairs on his own, so he wasn't forced to choose between being trapped upstairs or asking for help.

A specialized facility would have a team of medical staff, and other patients like him that can relate to his situation in a way the rest of his family can't. He'd have social interactions and a chance to build friendships. He might even live longer with better medical care.

I would have to ask him about it, but if that was what he wanted, then I couldn't hold him back. No matter how much the thought of letting go of my few remaining family members terrified me.

Noting my hesitation, D'Angelo backed

up. An odd, sad little laugh escaped him, and he ran a hand over his face.

"Ha. What am I doing? Offering such things like it's a trade... I'm basically trying to buy you."

He turned around and I heard him take a deep breath. I waited, but when he didn't immediately turn back toward me, I stepped around his body to face him instead.

His expression was hard, but his blue eyes glistened with a little extra moisture.

"I'm not being fair. After everything I've put you through, taking care of your family is the least I can do. Whether or not you agree to come with me, my offer still stands. Your family will be taken care of no matter what."

That took a little of the pressure off, to know that D'Angelo support was already assured, but that still left one very important question unanswered.

"Why?"

His hard expression twisted into confusion.

I stepped closer but didn't touch him.

"Why do you want me to come with you? What could you possibly get from me that you couldn't get anywhere else? I've never really understood from the beginning, but now that I know who you really are, I'm even more confused. Asking me to come with you is basically like asking me to live with you. That sounds like... that sounds like you want me to stay permanently."

This time D'Angelo was quick to respond, crossing the physical boundary between us and cupping my face in both hands. "I do. I want you to live with me and I want you to stay permanently. Honestly, I'd give anything for that. As for your other question 'why you?'..."

He leaned forward until our foreheads touched.

"Is it childish of me to say it feels like fate? I was born of an uncommon union between the Italian and Russian Mafia. I belong to both worlds, yet neither at the same time. Then I find out that you, someone who so perfectly matches my taste, have the same mix of blood flowing through your veins. It's like you were designed specifically for me."

It felt good to be held by him and absorb the warmth of his skin pressed against my own. Maybe it was foolish, but I couldn't imagine living without that comfort.

Feeling bold, I tipped my chin until our lips were almost touching. "One more question. What happens if I change my mind? If I come with you now, but decide it's not what I want later?"

"Of course I'd let you leave. I wouldn't want to keep you by force. If you decide that being with me isn't what you want, then you can return to your family, or anywhere else you'd rather go."

I smirked, and our lips brushed. "Then what have I got to lose?"

I kissed him, taking the initiative, but it didn't last long. Almost as soon as our mouths locked together, I felt his hunger and his passion ignite, and he took control of the kiss. His arms practically crushed me as they pulled me close.

It was to be expected. D'Angelo was a very intense person, and that translated to every aspect of his life, even intimacy.

Our kiss was abruptly cut off when D'Angelo pulled away, growling low under his breath. Then in one smooth motion, he picked me up and threw me over his shoulder.

I couldn't help the startled shout that was punched out of my lungs when my stomach curled over his shoulder. With my head hanging down toward the floor, I scrambled to grab anything I could reach, which ended up being his belt.

"Ah. D'Angelo. What're you doing?"

He laughed. A proper laugh this time. I couldn't see his expression, but the movement of his shoulders caused me to bounce a little.

"You asked what you had to lose. But this shouldn't be about loss. I'm reminding you what you have to gain."

It was no shock when he carried me toward the bedroom, though I pretended to protest anyway, beating my fists against his back.

"You brute. Put me down."

"As you wish."

He flipped me back over his shoulder, so I landed on the bed, breathless and dizzy.

"That... is not... what I meant."

"Oh, really..." He crawled onto the bed until he knelt over me. One finger tugged at the clasp to my pants. "Should have been more specific then."

Before he could get very far undoing my clothes, I grabbed the front of his shirt in two fists and pulled him closer, so my lips were beside his ear.

"How's this for specific. Fuck me this time. No toys. No messing around with our clothes still on. Take me properly."

I could feel his arousal pressing against my leg as he grinned down at me. "Tired of being a virgin?"

"For the love of God, yes." I started pulling his shirt open, and a few buttons may have hit the floor. He returned the favor, although not as wildly. My clothing escaped unharmed, but one way or another we were both eventually undressed.

The feeling of someone else's body pressed so fully against mine was still a novel experience. I was tempted to just rub myself against him, but that wasn't what I wanted. I wanted to feel claimed, all the way down to my core, like my very insides had been rewritten with his name.

When D'Angelo pulled away, I nearly snarled in frustration. "Where are you going? Come back."

"Just getting some things."

While I admired the view of him rooting through his closet, I would much rather have feasted with my hands than with my eyes.

He pulled out a familiar box and I groaned.

"I told you, no toys. Just you."

Laughing, he rejoined me on the bed and set the box aside.

"I know. I heard you. But we still need some supplies." From the box he pulled out a bottle of lube and a few condoms.

The lube he set next to us within easy reach, but the condom he placed in my hand.

"It's up to you. I'm clean, and I know you've never slept with anyone else before, but if you'd feel better with protection, we can still use it."

Contemplating the condom for a moment, I eventually tossed it aside. "If I can trust you with my life, then I can surely trust you with this."

He kissed me so hard that I fell back flat against the mattress. Clinging to his shoulders I breathed with him, trying to consume him as he consumed me. This lasted for several minutes, tongues dancing and lips passing whispered promises back and forth, before we parted, gasping for air. Even apart, we stayed close enough that a string of saliva still connected our lips.

One of his hands slipped down between my legs. At some point, while I'd been distracted, he'd coated two of his fingers in lube, which he now used to rub against my tight hole.

"Eeep." I jumped at the startling sensation of cold liquid against hot skin.

He kissed me again, much quicker this time. "Sorry. It'll warm up soon. Try to relax."

One of his fingers slipped inside me, and I arched my back as I dug my fingers into the meat of his shoulders.

"Relaxing is the last thing on my mind right now."

His finger inside me didn't hesitate. He slowly pressed it farther and farther, until eventually it was as deep as it could go.

I shivered and moaned low in the back of my throat when D'Angelo's finger brushed teasingly against my prostate, never quite pressing down.

He pressed a line of kisses against my throat. "If you don't relax, this is going to be a much rougher ride."

"I don't..." I gasped as a second finger breached my tight pucker, making its way inside me. "I don't think I can."

The second digit was soon as deep as

the first, and D'Angelo started scissoring the pair inside me, opening me up and giving my tense muscles no choice but to relax.

"Hmm?" D'Angelo sat up just enough to look down at me. "Fine then. Don't relax. I know you secretly like it rough."

He suddenly pulled his fingers out, leaving me heartbreakingly empty. I whined and writhed, desperate to be filled again. My own hand crept down between my legs, but before I could reach my goal, he grabbed both my wrists in an unyielding grip.

"Oh, no. You don't get to do that. Pleasuring you is my job." His smile turned dangerous. "If you can't control yourself, I'll have to help you out."

From the box, he grabbed a familiar length of nylon rope. I thought he was going to tie my hands to the headboard like last time, but instead he merely bound my wrists together. It didn't seem particularly effective when my arms were still free to move around, but then he gripped my shoulders and abruptly flipped me over, so I was lying on my stomach. My wrists were trapped under my own chest. Even if I wiggled my arms free and extended them above my head, it wouldn't do me any good. There was nothing useful to hold onto. At most, all I could do was hold the bed sheets with the tips of my fingers.

Grabbing my hips, D'Angelo pulled them up, so I was braced on my knees. The position drove my chest and shoulders harder into the mattress, which also trapped my wrists even more efficiently. Burying my face against the sheets, I tried to hide the sound of my desperate whimper.

"There," D'Angelo cooed as he slipped his fingers back inside me. "That's much better. Easier to reach."

He fingered me slowly at first, each movement smooth and deliberate as he coaxed me to open up for him. I continued to moan and whimper into the mattress as arousal built in my stomach and made my hips tremble.

Gradually, he began to speed up. His fingers plunged in and out of me faster and faster, until he was basically fucking me. My internal muscles automatically clenched down around the digits each time they pushed inside, trying to keep them there, and each time I was abandoned as they pulled out again.

"Such a little slut," he breathed against my skin as he bit my hip. "Already so desperate, and I'm not even actually inside you yet."

"Then hurry up," I panted, though my words were muffled against the mattress.

His laughter danced over my skin as a puff of air. "Such a tempting invitation."

I couldn't tell if he was sincere or mocking. At that point, I didn't care.

His fingers pulled out, and I groaned in disappointment, but he quickly pressed his hips against me. Shifting to get himself into just the right position, he brushed his cock against my puckered hole a few times, like he was asking for permission to enter.

I couldn't figure out how to form proper words, so I just moaned and pressed back against him. That seemed to do the trick.

One hand stroked my spine, like he was trying to calm me down, while the other gripped tightly to my hip to keep me in place. Very slowly, he pushed against me until the head of his cock slid inside my entrance, breaching the tight ring of muscles.

His cock was much bigger than a pair of fingers. It even felt bigger than the toy he'd used on me before. I trembled as he slowly forced my body to accommodate him, making space for himself inside me. Taking deep breaths, I focused on the feeling of slick skin and penetrating heat, the almost overwhelming sense of fullness. Pleasure burned up my spine, making my back arch, and I cried out when he hit a particularly sensitive spot deep inside me.

"There. Right there. Fuck."

His laughter sounded breathier than normal, like even he couldn't keep his composure.

"You get... mouthy when you're being fucked. Wonder if... you'll be able to keep that up."

Before I could reply, he pulled out much quicker than he'd entered the first time. Then, just before he was all the way out, he plunged back in. He set a quick pace, driving deep into my body over and over. His hips slapped against my ass cheeks, filling the room with the sound of slick skin and vicious panting. I began to babble as each trust made my brain short circuit.

"Fuck. Yes. I. There. Like. That." I was barely forming words let alone sentences, yet I also couldn't seem to stop.

D'Angelo leaned forward so he draped himself over my back, then picked up his pace. In this position, he couldn't pull as far out, but in return he was able to push even deeper.

I screamed into the mattress as my legs gave out, but an arm around my waist kept my hips in their upright angle. Kisses peppered the back of my neck, but I barely felt them. The feather light touches couldn't compete with the electric ecstasy running through my nerves.

There was no gradual build up like before. One moment, I still seemed far away from finding my end, and the next I was tumbling over the edge of orgasm like I'd been teleported. Every muscle in my body locked up, and I clung to the sheets below me with both fingers and toes.

D'Angelo kept thrusting for a moment, driving my climax higher until I felt so sensitive that it almost hurt. Then, pressing as deep into me as he could, he spilled into my ass. By then, I was already coming down from the high of my own peak, so the sudden heat that flooded me felt relaxing and nearly sent me to sleep.

We lay together for a few moments, both catching our breath. Once we were able to move again, D'Angelo slowly pulled out of me, which felt odd without raging hormones to distract me from the slimy texture against my skin.

I shuddered, but another kiss to my neck instantly soothed me.

Lying together in bed, he wrapped me in his arms as we both stared at the ceiling. The shadows had changed their angle, meaning a significant amount of time had passed, but I had no idea how long it had actually been.

Minutes?

Hours?

It didn't really matter.

"I need to leave in the next day or two," D'Angelo said, breaking the silence that had fallen over us.

"That's... quick."

His hand stroked my hair. "I understand if you need more time than that. I can't delay, but I can come back to collect you once you're ready to go. Assuming... you still want to."

Frowning, I threw a leg over his hip and pulled myself up until I sat atop his waist, and I was looking down at him for once. "Losing my virginity didn't change my mind about coming with you. In fact, I can probably be ready to go in two days. One of the good things about being poor. You don't have a lot of things to pack."

"Don't say things like that." D'Angelo sighed and ran a hand up my arm, tracing the scars there. "It makes me want to spoil you. Just wait. Soon you'll have closets full of fancy things. So much so, you won't even know what to do with everything."

"Yeah?" Grabbing his hand, I laced our fingers together. "Is that your love language? Gift giving?"

"Just... taking care of someone in general, I guess."

"Hmmm." Leaning down just far enough, I pressed a quick peck of a kiss to his lips. "So, you're saying you want to take care of me."

There was no hesitation in his voice when he responded. "Absolutely. You'll never want for anything."

Licking my lips and kissing him again, I kept my questions to myself.

How could he make that promise when I didn't even know what I wanted?

I wanted to focus on my art. That was obvious. But beyond that... I had no idea. My ambitions for life had never gone beyond taking care of my brother and keeping my family going day by day.

Maybe, it was time to set my sights on bigger goals.

Pouting, I sat up and lightly slapped his chest. "Well, you're already failing. I want a bath, and yet I'm not in a bath. You made a mess of me. I'm gross. Take responsibility."

I was only teasing. I didn't expect him to take it so seriously. But the moment the request was out of my mouth, he stood from the bed, literally picking me up in his arms, and carried me toward the bathroom.

"If you want a bath, then you'll get a bath. Anything you want, just ask for it. I'll take care of it."

Wrapping my arms around his neck, I leaned my head against him. "You'll take care of me?"

On the threshold between the bedroom and the bathroom, he stopped and pressed our foreheads together again.

"Of course. Always."

Dear Reader,

Thank you for reading Chasing Danger, book two in the Ruthless Empire series. For more morally gray alpha men who live and die by family loyalties and honor, and will unalive anyone who touches their man, snag your copy of book three, Kissing Danger.

If you enjoyed this book, please return to the online retailer where you made your purchase and leave me a review. Your thoughts may just encourage other readers to try my books, and help me continue writing the bad boys we all love. Even a few words means the world to me.
~Love, Evie Riley

OTHER BOOKS BY EVIE

Federal Protection Agency
Mason
Rafe
Ryzen
Cooper
Noah
Damien
Sebastian
Gabe
Logan

Ruthless Empire
Courting Danger
Chasing Danger
Kissing Danger

Smokejumpers
Hawke
Cyrus
Jase
Gage
Jackson
Xavier

Jasper Springs
Cade
Dawson
Drew
Grayson
Riley
Mitch

From The Edge
Shattered
Runaway
Jaded
Rescue
Hidden
Tormented

Gray Vale Pack
His Fated Mate
His Wounded Warrior
His Healing Heart

ABOUT THE AUTHOR

Evie Riley is a prolific, neurodivergent author known for her captivating MM romance novels. She has gained a significant following and topped the LGBT+ action and adventure bestseller charts with her series.

Evie's writing style often explores dark and gritty themes where her men must overcome difficult obstacles in their search for love, but she has also ventured into sweeter small-town romances, incorporating tropes like enemies-to-lovers, friends-to-lovers, age-gap, and forced proximity. She is known for crafting engaging romantic suspense novels and has a knack for creating interconnected series worlds that keep readers invested.

Interestingly, Ms. Riley has hinted at exploring new genres, such as Alien Omegaverse Romance, in the future.

Outside of writing, she enjoys spending time at the beach and has a quirky personality, described by her partner as ranging from cute to deadly, depending on her blood-chocolate levels.

Evie spends her nights writing bad boys in love, and her days wrangling the sweet boys she loves.

www.ingramcontent.com/pod-product-compliance
Lightning Source LLC
Chambersburg PA
CBHW071402200726
48294CB00002B/274